A CATERED AFFAIR

Jean, my cousin,
To Love a Happy Endings!

A CATERED
AFFAIR

•

Carolyn Matkowsky

Savor the romance...
Carolyn Matkowsky
March 2003

AVALON BOOKS
NEW YORK

PRINTED IN THE UNITED STATES OF AMERICA
ON ACID-FREE PAPER
BY HADDON CRAFTSMEN, BLOOMSBURG, PENNSYLVANIA

This book is dedicated to the Rosebud Critique Group—
Gwen, Mary Lou, Ruth Ellen, and Susan—
for their help and encouragement and unwavering belief in me.
Thank you to my loyal writing friends—
Dottie, Linda, Lisa, and Sue, to my sister Linda
for her support and enthusiasm, and to Joe and Joey
for their love.

Chapter One

"**Y**ou offered our company to Sackett Industries? Gail, how could you? I'd rather go under than sell to them." Mary Beth Kendrick smoothed an unsteady hand over her hair and glared at her friend and business partner.

Gail O'Connell folded her arms across her chest and glared back. "Get your redheaded temper under control. We will go under unless we do something fast. As equal partner, I can't sell without you, but I refuse to just lie down and die. I thought you were more of a fighter too."

Gail's tirade brought quick tears to Mary Beth's eyes and she turned to face the window. Pedestrians hurried by in the spring sunshine on the street outside their catering shop. How could they look so happy

1

when her world was crumbling like a piece of stale cake?

A few hours ago their biggest client had cancelled. Now this. Tom Sackett. She'd heard he was back in town. Wasn't it enough that he'd humiliated her so badly years before?

"Mary Beth?"

She let out a deep sigh and turned at Gail's touch on her arm. Gail didn't know what Tom had once meant to her. She couldn't take her anger and frustration out on her friend. "I'm sorry. It's been a real bad day."

Mary Beth walked to one of the large chintz chairs and sank into the thick cushions. She gripped the chair arms, finding no comfort in the satin smoothness of the fabric. Her gaze scanned the small reception area with its flowered drapes and chairs, pale greens and peaches. An English country garden, the decorator had said. More like an abandoned garden now. A new competitor had blown into town six months ago and plucked all the flowers, leaving them with the weeds . . . and lots of bills. Even the usually soothing lavender potpourri seemed to have lost its potency.

The kitchen in the back was state of the art—all gleaming white and stainless steel. And rarely used. They'd had such hopes when they moved into these new, upscale quarters and expanded their business. Now, a year later, they had few customers and almost no money.

Gail plopped into a chair opposite her. "The financial officer from Sackett approached me while you were at your mother's. He said they wanted to invest in some small businesses and ours had potential." Her dimples flashed in a fleeting smile. "You have to agree we have potential."

Gail raked her fingers through her curly blond hair, her expression serious again. "We're in hock to our eyeballs. I used up all of Pete's and my savings. You used all your money. None of the banks will give us a loan. We can declare bankruptcy and admit defeat. Is that what you want?"

"Of course it's not what I want," Mary Beth said, rubbing her aching temples. "We've poured our blood and guts into this place. I don't even mind the killer hours, because it's our company, our dream." She blew her breath out. "I have no appetite for going back to taking orders from chefs who just want to get the food out, assembly-line style. But I can't sell to Sackett. Anybody but them."

She could see tight lines etched around Gail's mouth. "Why not?" Gail said. "Sackett is one of the strongest companies in Delaware. They're offering us a chance to stay free, to make our dream come true."

"I know that," Mary Beth said. "It's just . . . I went to high school with Tom Sackett." Saying his name boiled the old feelings of love, hope, and betrayal into a stew of conflicting emotions, tightening her stomach.

"That's good, right?" Puzzlement colored Gail's voice.

"We didn't part friends. I can't forget what Tom did. I don't trust him."

"Suppose you tell me about it," Gail said.

"I can't," Mary Beth replied, shaking her head. To dredge up the past would force her to relive the old pains she'd fought so hard to overcome. She couldn't.

"Don't pull the stubborn act on me. Our future depends on this." Gail shot her a look filled with determination and quiet desperation.

Guilt stabbed at Mary Beth's gut. She owed Gail. A lot. Clasping her hands tightly together, she took a deep breath.

"Tom belonged to the rich, cool crowd at St. Anselm's Prep," Mary Beth said. "I attended on a hardship grant. I fell in love with him when I tutored him in English junior year. We started dating in the middle of senior year. It bothered me that we never went out with his friends. I wondered if they even knew about us, but I was so crazy for him, I shrugged off my doubts.

"When Tom asked me to the graduation formal, I was ecstatic. I figured he must care for me too and he was ready to tell the world. Was I ever wrong." She blinked away tears.

"What happened?" Gail asked softly.

Mary Beth pressed her trembling hands against her stomach and fought for calmness. "We had fun that night. At first. Tom and I danced and laughed. I ignored the snickers and sly looks from his friends. He took me out to the patio where we could be alone. We kissed."

Bittersweet sorrow spread through her. "A magical kiss filled with love, hope, and dreams. I told him I loved him and wanted to spend my life with him." She chewed on her lip. "To this day, I can't believe I said that. It makes me want to gag."

"You were a teenager," Gail said. "Young girls tend to be melodramatic. What did Tom say?"

"Nothing; he didn't have to. His friends said it for him." Anger made the bile rise again in Mary Beth's throat.

"What do you mean?" Gail asked.

"He set me up. We weren't alone. His friends stood watching. When I made my lovesick declaration, they clapped and laughed. Cash changed hands as bets were paid off. I've always wondered how much money Tom made off my torment."

Mary Beth swiped at a tear as it rolled down her cheek. Her stomach twisted with anger and sadness for the naive young girl who'd been so in love, and so brutally used.

Gail leaned over and placed one of her hands on Mary Beth's. "Honey, I'm so sorry. That was cruel. Did Tom ever apologize?"

Mary Beth shook her head. "I left for the beach with my mom the next day. We planned to stay with my aunt while I looked for a summer job. I haven't seen Tom since that night."

Gail's hand tightened over hers. "Maybe he tried to call you but there was no one at your house."

"I stopped torturing myself with maybes long ago," Mary Beth said.

"Do you still love him?"

"No!" Mary Beth yanked her hand away.

Gail studied her. "They say living well is the best revenge. Show Tom the strong, independent woman you've become. Listen to what Sackett has to offer. If we refuse to even talk to them, Tom's cruelty twelve years ago will hurt you all over again. And he will still have power over you."

Mary Beth tugged on her braid where it rested on her shoulder. Did she have the strength to face Tom again, to reopen the wounds that had bled her heart dry so many years before?

She glanced at Gail. Her friend was right. They had to fight to keep their dream alive. She wasn't a trembling teenager anymore. Tom couldn't hurt her again.

Gail's gray gaze held hers. "Mary Beth, if we lose this place and you can't find a job right away, how will you support your mother and pay her medical bills?"

"I don't know," Mary Beth said.

A mischievous glint came into Gail's eyes. "If you can't afford your apartment, you'll have to move in with your mother."

"You play dirty, Gail."

"I know which buttons to push."

Mary Beth sighed. "Okay, we'll talk to Sackett.

Tom might not even be involved. He probably has others do the work for him."

"Oh," Gail said.

"Oh, what?"

"They want to meet with us tomorrow."

"They?" Mary Beth arched an eyebrow.

Gail's cheeks turned pink and she glanced away. "That financial guy. And Tom Sackett."

"Nice place you have here."

Mary Beth jumped at the sound of the deep male voice behind her. Water from the pot she was filling sloshed onto the floor. She jerked the faucet shut and gripped the counter edge.

His voice. Richer, mellowed. Warming her with old memories, old yearnings. She was eighteen again. In love. Dreaming of a life spent by his side. Until he betrayed her.

Anger jolted her like boiling liquid spilling on her lap. Biting down on her lip, Mary Beth turned slowly to face Tom Sackett.

He filled the doorway, his masculine power reaching out, drawing her in as it always had. Despite his aristocratic breeding and elegantly tailored suit, he still had the look of the renegade about him. His thick black hair curled around his ears and trailed down his neck, a trifle too long. The hot, deep blue of his eyes scorched her.

She lifted her chin and willed starch into her spine. "You're early," she said, glancing at the clock. "The meeting isn't for another half hour. My partner's not here yet."

He arched an eyebrow. "Hello to you too. That's not much of a greeting after twelve years."

She placed a hand on her hip. "As I recall, our last meeting was less than cordial."

He tightened his jaw. "People change, Mary Beth."

"Do they?"

"Believe it." The determined set of his rugged features stopped any further argument. "Do you want to talk about it?" he asked.

"No." She tugged on her braid, trying to gain control of her emotions. For the sake of her company, she wouldn't let her feelings interfere. "We have a business deal to negotiate. Nothing more."

Tom's harsh features softened. His gaze scanned her face, making her wonder if her tension showed. "You're more beautiful than I remembered."

Awareness and a flash of anger tightened her stomach. She dug her nails into her palms. "Saving my company is my primary concern."

"Mine too," he said. "A businessman expects a return on his investment." He strode into the kitchen with the confidence born of inherited wealth and family standing.

Squaring her shoulders, Mary Beth fought the onslaught of old hurts. She'd grown up in the years since he'd humiliated her. Her family might not have his social connections, but her poverty-stricken upbringing had made her strong. Strong enough to fight for her professional life and keep her pride—and her heart—intact.

"Coffee smells good. May I have a cup?" Tom straddled one of the high stools surrounding the white-tiled center island.

Glad to do something to distract her from past memories and Tom's disturbing presence, she grabbed a heavy white mug from the counter and poured a steaming cup of vanilla almond coffee. "Just cream, right?"

"You remembered," he said.

"A lucky guess," she replied, handing him the mug. His fingers grazed hers as he took it, sending heat racing up her arm.

She escaped to the opposite side of the kitchen and leaned against the counter. The citrus scent of his cologne lingered in her nostrils, stirring up the unwanted memory of their kiss at the formal. But the sweet kiss that had promised love and dreams fulfilled had been tainted with betrayal.

A new dread suddenly filled her. "I won't take charity, Tom. If this is about payback, there will be no deal."

She chewed her lip at her overly dramatic words. Seeing Tom again peeled away the years, bringing out the teenager in her. She had to get a grip.

He stared at her over the rim of his mug and took a quick sip before banging the cup on the counter. Coffee spilled over the sides onto the clean white tile.

"I'm a lawyer and a businessman. I don't gamble

with my firm's money." The intensity in his sapphire eyes held her motionless. "I've checked your company out," he continued. "Talked to people. You have the potential to be big, but you're over-extended. That's where Sackett comes in. We'll help you get on your feet. You have to look successful to be successful."

Mary Beth angled her chin toward him, still not ready to believe him. "Sackett Industries doesn't invest in small businesses like ours."

He shrugged and swallowed more coffee. "Sackett owns a diverse portfolio of companies. Catering will mesh well with our other holdings. We do a lot of corporate entertaining. We could use an in-house caterer."

She studied him, trying to assess the truth of his words. The confident set of his jaw spoke of a strength and maturity eighteen-year-old Tom had lacked. Maybe he had changed after all.

Stop it, her brain shouted. Dreams of Tom had only caused her pain in the past. She couldn't go down that path again.

She grabbed the coffeepot and quickly poured some for herself. Hot liquid splashed on her hand, scalding her. She jumped.

"Are you okay?" The stool scraped the floor as Tom stood up and started toward her.

"I'm fine," she rasped, waving him away. She didn't want him close to her, not while she felt so vulnerable . . . and angry. Angry at him and at the circumstances that had brought him into her life again. She jerked on the faucet and held her hand under cold water.

"This kitchen is great," he said. "I'm planning to renovate mine. Maybe you could come over sometime and give me your professional opinion."

"I don't think so." She wiped her hands on a towel and faced him. "If we work out a deal today—and I'm not at all sure about that—I will not be at your beck and call to help decorate your house, or perform any other duties."

"You always did have too much pride for your own good," he said quietly.

She met his gaze and held it, refusing to look away despite the small seed of awareness that grew in her. "Pride got me through school and it will get me through this. I won't be dependent on you, or anyone, for long."

He quirked his mouth into a wry smile. "A little bit of overreaction, Mary Beth?"

She tugged on her braid. The man had a way of making her lose her cool.

"Hi—I'm not late, am I?"

They both started as Gail bounded into the room, her blond curls dancing around her delicate face.

Gail looked from Tom to Mary Beth.

"You're not late. He's early." Mary Beth nodded toward Tom.

"Tom Sackett," he said, holding out his hand.

"Gail O'Connell. I'm the 'and Company' in Kendrick and Company Caterers and Party Planners."

He laughed. "Glad to meet you." His quick smile made Gail's cheeks dimple with pleasure.

Resentment knifed through Mary Beth. Tom could charm the apples out of a fresh-baked pie.

"How's Joey?" Mary Beth blurted out.

"His fever broke now that the antibiotics have kicked in." Gail pulled her hand from Tom's. "Joey is my five-year-old," she explained. "My husband is out of town and I had trouble finding a sitter. Sorry to keep you waiting."

"No problem. My financial officer's not here yet." Tom sat on the stool. "I got here early to check out the place and talk over old times with Mary Beth."

Mary Beth widened her eyes. *Old times?* Hardly times she'd want to reminisce about. The future, her company's future, was all that mattered now.

Gail threw her a look. She ignored it.

"We should get ready for the meeting," Mary Beth said, opening one of the cabinets and pulling out a teak tray.

"Coffee smells good," Gail said. "I'll get the petit fours."

Gail took the plate of dainty cakes from the refrigerator and set them on the counter in front of Tom. "I'm the pastry chef. Mary Beth couldn't bake her way out of a burning oven, but the girl sure can cook."

"Mary Beth always did everything well," Tom said. "Her intelligence scared the heck out of me in school. So did her beauty." His gaze, hot as a blue flame, locked with Mary Beth's. She looked quickly away.

"There will be four of us at the meeting, right?" Mary Beth said. She set mugs and a carafe on the tray. Keeping busy would distract her mind from Tom . . . and from the overwhelming sadness and frustration that the business she had struggled to conceive and build might owe its survival to the man who had mortally wounded her heart.

She groaned inwardly. She was thinking like an over-dramatic teen again. Maybe Tom hadn't mortally wounded her, but his betrayal had kept her from trusting any man, although she had had two serious relationships since him.

"How long have you two been partners?" Tom asked. The cool tone of his voice made Mary Beth glance at him. The rigid set of his handsome features gave no hint of the longing that had softened them a minute ago.

She let her breath out, convinced that tension had her imagination working overtime. Tom didn't care for her, had never cared for her.

She poured coffee into the carafe, concentrating on the steady stream of hot liquid and trying to ignore the small drips of hurt that seemed to burn her heart.

Having Tom here exposed the raw emotions of the young, lovestruck girl she'd once been. Straightening her spine, she willed the teenage Mary Beth back, deep inside her, where she belonged.

"To answer your question," Gail said, "as my usually vocal partner seems to have lost her voice, we've been friends since college and we attended the Culinary Institute together. Mary Beth opened the business two years ago and I bought in six months later. Here, try one of these." She pushed the plate of pastries toward him.

Tom popped a small cake into his mouth. His eyes widened. The surprised pleasure on his face made the two women exchange grins.

"Wow!" He licked his lips.

Mary Beth's knees wobbled like half-set gelatin. She gripped the counter for support and stared at Tom's mouth. What would it be like to kiss him again?

Their eyes met. Awareness sizzled and crackled between them, charging the atmosphere like downed power lines after a storm.

"Cakes are good, huh?" Gail said, laughing.

Mary Beth blinked her eyes, breaking the connection with Tom.

"My husband, Pete, gained ten pounds the first couple of months after I entered the business. He was our official taster. He gave up the job and joined the gym."

Bless Gail for rambling, Mary Beth thought. She fingered the gold chain at her neck and took calming breaths, trying to diffuse the attraction arcing between her and Tom.

"Can I apply for the position?" Tom's words teased, but his voice was husky and his gaze lingered on Mary Beth.

"We wouldn't want you to ruin your manly physique," Gail said.

Mary Beth's gaze seemed to have a will if its own, attaching itself to Tom's broad shoulders. The designer cut of his expensive suit couldn't disguise the width of his chest or the barely leashed power of his muscles under the finely woven wool jacket and silk shirt. She swallowed around the lump in her throat.

"I'll get the papers from the office," Mary Beth said, hurrying from the room.

"Well, that's done." Mary Beth put her feet on the oak coffee table in the reception area. With the pleated shades drawn, the only light came from the small Tiffany lamp on the side table. The room reflected her mood, somber and shadowed. She swiped at a tear. "I feel like I've signed away my firstborn."

Gail sighed. "You're the one who gave birth to this baby. Even though I'm just the foster mother, I feel bad."

"When you bought in, you became an equal partner," Mary Beth said. "You love this business as much as I do."

"And it's just as heart-wrenching to lose it." Gail tucked a blond curl behind her ear.

Mary Beth leaned her head back on the cushioned chair and closed her eyes. "At least we still own a small portion and we've got creative license."

"Sackett Industries was surprisingly fair," Gail said.

"They know better than to change a winning recipe." Mary Beth sat up and looked at Gail, sitting opposite her. She twisted her braid around her hand.

"A year ago we were the new darlings on the block, with more business than we could handle, and now we don't even have controlling interest in our own company. How did we let this happen?"

"Maybe we got too sure of ourselves," Gail said, shaking her head. "We ignored those 'flash and dash' caterers when they breezed in, bringing their glitzy Philadelphia style."

"Their food is terrible," Mary Beth said. "Remember the roast beef at the Larson wedding? And they use canned mushrooms. Ugh. But people don't seem to notice."

"Because they're fooled by the pretty wrappings," Gail said. "Some people would rave over cardboard if it were wrapped fancy. Now with Sackett's money and influence, we can give them glitter too. Only we have substance behind our packaging."

"Sackett," Mary Beth said in a low voice. Tom. Appealing. Dangerous. Her boss.

She tightened her jaw. "This is only a temporary situation. As soon as we can, we'll buy our business back. I will not be dependent on any man, especially Tom Sackett."

Gail put a hand up. "Don't bite my head off. Since I've known you, you've had this thing about making your own way. You've scared off a lot of good men with your stubborn self-reliance. Maybe you should loosen up a little."

"Never," Mary Beth said, pulling on her braid. "Besides, I wouldn't want a man I could intimidate."

Gail quirked her mouth into a grin. "Maybe you've met your match."

"What do you mean?"

"Tom," Gail said. "He impressed me in the meeting. He's strong, forceful, a take-charge kind of guy. And he's fair. I like him."

"I told you what he did to me," Mary Beth said. "He's not the paragon of virtue you think."

"He was eighteen. People grow up."

"What would Pete say if he knew how outrageously you flirted with Tom?" Mary Beth asked.

Gail waved her hand in the air. "Pete knows I love him. And I wasn't flirting. I was just responding to a delicious hunk with a killer smile."

Mary Beth's heart constricted. So what if Gail found Tom attractive? She didn't care what other women thought of him.

"And you, my dear, sprouted green horns," Gail said.

"What?" Mary Beth bolted upright.

"Don't act the innocent with me." Gail's eyes crinkled with amusement. "I wasn't in the room two minutes when you asked about Joey. You wanted to be sure Tom knew I was married, and therefore unavailable." Gail crossed her arms, a smug look on her face.

"Joey is my godson. I'm concerned about him. And *you* brought up the subject of your husband, not me."

"I know you care about Joey," Gail said. "But the way you blurted it out was a little obvious, although

I don't think Tom noticed. Men are clueless about those things."

"I don't know what you're talking about." Mary Beth shifted uncomfortably, wishing she could ignore the inner voice that screamed Gail was right.

Unable to sit still, Mary Beth jumped from the chair and stalked to the window. The truth of Gail's words was hard to digest.

She rubbed her forehead as if she could rub away the confusion tumbling around her mind. Tom meant nothing to her, nothing at all.

Pulling up one of the shades, she stared out. The street lamps cast a pale light on the dusk-filled sidewalk. Like her life now: pale shadows with no clear definition.

Sirens cut the quiet, adding an edge and danger to the air. Tom was like the sirens. Dangerous. Ready to wreak havoc on her heart.

She straightened. She would never let him get close enough to hurt her again.

"Mary Beth?" Gail stood behind her. "I was just teasing. I didn't realize Tom still means something to you."

She whirled around to face Gail. "He means nothing more than a business arrangement. Tom Sackett may have supplied the ingredients to get our careers cooking again, but he has no other place in my life."

"Okay," Gail said, shrugging. A grin split her face. "Why are we acting like doom? We're back in business. Give me a high five!"

Smiling, Mary Beth exchanged high fives with Gail. "Let's toast with that gourmet cider we've been saving," Mary Beth said. "Those upstart caterers may have stolen our customers, but we're taking them back, and theirs too. We'll show this town what real cooks are made of."

"Way to go," Gail said, leading them into the kitchen. "With Sackett financing us we'll be the toast of Wilmington. And we'll make tons of money."

"And we'll buy our company back." Mary Beth clenched her hands into fists. She would take care of herself. She wouldn't end up like her mother.

The traffic from Delaware into Pennsylvania was heavy for a Thursday evening. Tom rubbed his hand on the back of his neck to relieve his aching muscles.

He should have bought a house in Wilmington near the family. But after his years in New York City, he wanted peace, solitude, country. The rolling hills of nearby Chadds Ford suited him perfectly.

How much peace would he have now that he'd seen Mary Beth Kendrick again? Cat Eyes. What would she do if she knew his secret name for her? He smiled. Probably slash his face.

She'd always been a spitfire. A red-haired dynamo with flashing green eyes and full, soft lips that begged him to kiss her.

Memories of kissing Mary Beth burned him, making him tighten his grip on the wheel. Their kiss at the formal had been something else. Special. Filled with longing. Her sweetness and wide-eyed trust had filled him with pride and a need to protect her and hold her close forever. He had known before she said the words that she loved him.

And then the others ruined it. He hadn't known they were there, watching. He should have gone after her. But anger and stunned disbelief had choked him. Despite how hard he'd tried to overcome the barriers between them, she was so ready to believe the worst of him that she'd fled before he'd had a chance to explain.

His own selfish fears had frozen him too and he'd let her run away, out of his life. And then there was the accident. By the time his dad was out of danger and he could think again, Mary Beth was gone. The accusation and hurt in her eyes that night still haunted him.

He'd spent the past twelve years proving his worth to the world, to himself, making amends for the spoiled, arrogant, wild kid he'd once been.

Only one person's opinion mattered at this moment. He hadn't realized Mary Beth still harbored such resentment. The fight would be harder than he had anticipated, but he would earn her respect and forgiveness.

Tom slammed on his brakes, almost colliding with the car in front of him. The other driver made a rude gesture. Tom shrugged. He needed to concentrate on the road and not let thoughts of Mary Beth distract him.

He twisted his mouth into a wry smile. She'd been distracting him since the first time he saw her in the school hall when he was fourteen. He'd bumped into a door, mesmerized by her green cat eyes and her thick red-gold braid.

He owned her company, but he'd never own her heart. A pang of regret hit him, as he focused back on the road.

Chapter Two

"I can't believe you bought a catering business." Maureen Sackett DiMauro heaved her seven-months pregnant body out of the leather chair and rounded her desk to face Tom. "I hope you know what you're doing."

Tom gritted his teeth and prayed for patience. Maureen might be a foot shorter than he, but as older sister, she still liked to flex her authority "muscles."

"I know what I'm doing, and calm down or you'll have that baby right now," he said.

"It's my third pregnancy." Maureen patted her stomach. "This fella's not going anywhere for a while."

She settled her deep blue gaze on Tom. "I'm AVP and I had to find out about your latest venture from my secretary. Have you at least told Dad?"

Tom rolled his eyes. "Of course Dad knows. I am acquisitions director. He doesn't interfere with my decisions. And you would have found out about it at the board meeting next week."

Maureen waved her hand in the air. "You're the prodigal son, returned to the fold. You can do no wrong as far as Dad's concerned." She arched an eyebrow. "Humor me. My hormones are surging. Explain how a catering business will benefit Sackett."

"Sit down and I'll tell you. You make me nervous, standing up in your condition." Tom pushed her gently into one of the upholstered chairs in her office at Sackett Industries and perched himself on the desk, facing her.

Maureen folded her arms on her protruding stomach and narrowed her eyes. Her black hair swung softly around her face.

"You always look most beautiful when you're pregnant," Tom said. "Robert is a lucky man."

"Don't throw the charm at me. I'm immune. Start talking." Despite her words, Maureen's generous mouth tilted into a grin.

"An in-house caterer makes perfect sense," Tom said. He picked up a sterling silver pen from the desk and rolled it between his fingers, enjoying the cool smoothness of the metal. "We've got the monthly board meeting, the quarterly directors' meeting; we'll save money by having our own caterer plus earn Sackett a reputation as a class act."

"But. . . ."

He held up his hand, silencing her. "Hear me out. You and Robert entertain clients, as do Mom and Dad. I plan to do some business entertaining myself." The picture of Mary Beth working in his kitchen, thick braid swinging and green eyes flashing, sped through his mind. He shifted uncomfortably and laid the pen on the desk. Sunlight bounced off the silver, making the pen seem to wink at him.

"That's all well and good," Maureen said. "But will Sackett make money from this deal? Is the business viable? Did you check it out?"

"I'm not a complete idiot, Maureen. I am an officer in this organization. And a lawyer. Kendrick and Company has the potential to be the premier caterer in this area. The two owners have a solid business plan with a clear focus. They're graduates of the Culinary Institute. I hear their food is exceptional." He loosened his tie and smiled at her. "I know they make outstanding pastry."

"Kendrick. That name sounds familiar," Maureen said. There was a knock on the door. "Ms. DiMauro, can I interrupt for a minute?"

"Come in Rose," she called to her secretary.

"I'm sorry, but these letters have to be signed right away so I can get them out in today's mail," the middle-aged woman said, entering the office.

While Maureen reviewed the letters and conferred with her secretary, Tom strode to the large window that dominated the room. He stared outside to the pond filled with geese. The fowl were no doubt enjoying the spring sunshine. He envied them their oblivion. No beautiful redhead invaded their dreams at night, filling them with visions of what could never be.

His gaze wandered the rolling hills, pale green with new grass and dotted with pink- and white-blossomed dogwoods. Sackett Industries headquarters sprawled over fifty acres of prime suburban real estate. It felt good to be home. He'd made the right decision to come back and take his place in the family business. His parents needed him. The years had taken their toll on them. His dad's limp, the result of the accident so long ago, seemed more pronounced every day.

His time away had taught him a lot, matured him. He had finally buried the shallow, privileged kid who just wanted to party. The kid who stood by, doing nothing, while others' vicious words and actions hurt a friend.

His thoughts cut to the day before, at Kendrick and Company. Mary Beth. She had weathered the cruelty and kept her pride and dignity intact. Would he ever be worthy of her?

The office door closed softly. He heard Maureen fidgeting in her chair, but he continued to watch the geese swimming placidly. He wished his own life could be as calm, but seeing Mary Beth again had thrown him into a storm. He could never mean more to her than an unwanted business partner. Regret squeezed his heart.

"Of course!" Maureen exclaimed. "There was a

Mary Beth Kendrick in your class at St. Anselm's. Is it her company?"

Tom turned to his sister. "She's one of the owners."

Maureen tapped her bottom lip with her finger. "I remember her. Pretty little thing. Red hair. Always wore it in a braid. Didn't she tutor you?"

"Junior year English," he said. "I partied too much and my grades slipped. She helped me." Self-loathing roiled his stomach. *And I let her down,* he thought.

"She was so intense," Maureen said. "I never saw her smile."

"Then you missed something special. Mary Beth's smile lights up the world. There's no one quite like her."

Maureen's eyes widened. "You're in love with her."

Tom tensed. "Don't be ridiculous. She's just an old friend who needs help." He let his breath out. "Besides, she hates my guts."

"I doubt that she hates you," Maureen said, smiling. "I knew there had to be more to this catering deal." She patted her stomach. "The last two months of a pregnancy are usually so tedious, but this is going to be fun."

"Fun? What are you talking about?"

Maureen grinned. "There's Mary Beth. Just an old friend, you say, which I don't believe for a minute. And Taylor Bennett's back in town."

Tom groaned. "Taylor? I thought she lived in Princeton. And Mary Beth and I are business partners, nothing more."

"Protest all you want," Maureen said, "but I know you well. As for Taylor, when she heard you were home, she hightailed it back here as fast as her pretentious little stilettos could move. She still wants to get her well-manicured hooks into you. I thought you had a thing for her once."

He shrugged. "We dated for a little while in school. I outgrew Taylor a long time ago."

"Well, she's apparently never outgrown you." Maureen relaxed in her chair and grinned like the proverbial cat that swallowed the canary and had another one stashed away. "I'm going to sit back and enjoy the show," she said.

"What show?" Tom glared at his sister.

Her smile grew wider. "You want Mary Beth. Taylor wants you. What does Mary Beth want?"

"Kendrick and Company Caterers and Party Planners."

Mary Beth smiled at the clipped British voice coming from the reception area. Their new secretary added a touch of class to the place.

She sighed contentedly and scanned the gleaming kitchen. Sunlight streamed into the room, reflecting off the stainless steel of the commercial refrigerator. A catchy Beach Boys tune played on the radio.

All was right with her world, she thought, as she rhythmically chopped celery. The familiar weight of her favorite knife soothed her.

She sighed again. Her world wasn't completely

right. She no longer owned her business. But that was just a temporary setback. And then there was Tom. Was he temporary too? Just thinking of him made her heart do a little dance that she quickly squashed.

He hadn't been around in the two weeks since they'd closed the deal. Maybe he intended to keep a low profile. That was okay with her—the less she saw him, the better. No constant reminders of the past. She could pretend that she wasn't financially dependent on Tom.

Dependent on Tom. Her chest constricted. She brought the knife down hard on the celery.

"Trying to kill those vegetables?"

Mary Beth let out a little scream and jumped back. The knife clattered to the tiled floor.

She faced Tom. "Must you always sneak up on me like that?"

He leaned against the door frame with his arms folded across his chest and a grin on his chiseled features.

"You really need to work on your hellos, Mary Beth."

"Maybe you should quit sneaking up on me."

"From now on I'll have Mrs. Hagerty announce me from the other room." He threw her a devastating smile guaranteed to charm women from eight to eighty.

All except her, she thought, angling her chin. So what if he looked achingly handsome with his shirt-sleeves rolled up to his elbows, exposing muscular, tanned arms sprinkled with black hairs. His loosened tie and ruffled hair made him look younger, carefree, vulnerable.

Oh, no, she thought, looking quickly away. *I will not fall victim to his appeal again. Look what happened the first time.*

She retrieved her knife and dipped it in soapy water. She scrubbed it hard, as if she could scrub Tom out of her life.

"I thought chefs revered their knives," he said. "You look like you want to harm yours."

Mary Beth rinsed the knife and set it on the counter. Calmer now and feeling in control, she wiped her hands on a paper towel and turned to Tom.

"Is this a professional visit to check on your investment?" she asked.

"Yes and no." He stepped into the kitchen. "Curtis keeps me up-to-date on our subsidiaries. I've been busy closing another deal. I had a little free time and I thought I'd stop by and see how my two favorite caterers are doing. How's Mrs. Hagerty working out, by the way?"

"Barbara's a wonderful secretary. Thank you for sending her to us. She's organized and efficient. I think her accent alone has won us customers." Despite her feelings about Tom, Mary Beth had to admit that his financial backing and subtle hints and suggestions, communicated by Mr. Curtis, had brought them new business and taken their company to the next level.

"Smells great in here," Tom said, sniffing the air.

"What's cooking?" He walked over to the side counter and lifted the cloth covering the dough Gail had set out to rise. "Homemade bread. One of my favorites," he said. "What's in the oven?"

"Lamb," she said, opening the oven door to check on the succulent meat. The pungent odor of rosemary and cinnamon wafted through the room. "We're making lamb stew, but we like to roast the meat first. It gives the stew a better flavor."

"Lamb stew in May?" Tom grabbed a stool from under the center island and straddled it. "What kind of job do you have?"

Mary Beth tucked a stray curl behind her ear and leaned against the counter. The clicking sounds of computer keys came from the reception room. Paul McCartney singing a romantic ballad flowed from the radio.

And Tom sat before her, looking appealing, dangerous, and completely at home in a kitchen. How did he manage that?

"Mary Beth? Who is the dinner for?"

Embarrassment heated her cheeks. "Sorry. I have a lot on my mind."

"Evidently." His crooked grin warmed her like a glass of hot cider on a cold day.

Clenching her hands, she thrust them into her apron pockets. "We're catering an engagement dinner tonight for an attorney and her fiancé. It's a small party. Only six people. The hostess wants lamb stew and homemade bread."

Tom frowned. "Why lamb stew?"

Mary Beth shrugged. "We tried to talk her into something lighter, like angel-hair pasta with shrimp sauce, but she and her fiancé shared lamb stew the day they met, in a ski lodge in the Poconos. They wanted to recreate that."

"Kind of romantic," he said.

"I suppose so, if you go for that sort of thing."

He arched an eyebrow. "You're not a romantic, I take it."

"I have no time for romance, nor do I want it. Being a romantic can set a person up for all kinds of hurt."

Their gazes locked. Pain flickered in Tom's eyes. What woman had put that pain there? Jealousy and regret stirred in Mary Beth. She tightened her jaw.

Breaking the connection, she glanced at the clock. "If I don't hurry and finish, there won't be a meal." She grabbed her knife and began cutting the mushrooms she had set aside earlier.

"Where's Gail?" he asked.

"At Joey's school for a class party. She should be back soon. Gail usually acts as my sous-chef."

"Give me an apron and tell me what to do."

Widening her eyes, she looked at him. "You? Cook?"

He laughed. "Hey, give me credit for not being a complete slacker."

She couldn't help smiling.

"You should smile more often," he said softly. "You look even more beautiful, if that's possible."

Her face felt as hot as the oven. "I'll get you an apron," she said, going to the closet and pulling out a crisp chef's apron.

He donned the garment and rubbed his hands together. "I'm ready. What do you need done?"

She swallowed and stared at him. No man had the right to look that virile wearing a large white apron.

He frowned. "What do you need, Mary Beth?"

"Potatoes," she said, fumbling in a drawer for a paring knife. "I need potatoes."

"Okay," he said. "That's a start."

"Here." She thrust the knife at him. "Can you peel those potatoes in that bowl over there?"

"Sure. I'm a whiz at peeling."

Mary Beth turned back to chopping the mushrooms, needing the methodical, familiar task to help unravel her tangled emotions.

"You need all of these peeled?" he asked.

"Yes, please, unless you're not up to the job."

"I think I can handle this," he said, chuckling.

They worked in silence. The sound of her rhythmic cutting was broken by the occasional plop of a potato into the bowl.

She'd worked in countless kitchens with a multitude of partners, but never had such ordinary tasks like chopping and peeling been tinged with the electricity that crackled between her and Tom.

Mary Beth absorbed the heady warmth like exotic spices dropped in simmering broth. For just a little while she'd give in to the deep yearnings she'd long suppressed.

Oldies played on the radio and sunlight warmed the bright room. If she closed her eyes, she would be transported back in time. To chem lab, working as partners with Tom. He made her laugh so hard once that they were both thrown out of class. She smiled. It was the only time she'd ever gotten into trouble in school.

Then there was junior year English. She shook her head at the memory. She had taken her job as tutor so seriously. Tom just wanted to have fun. That was the young Tom . . . fun, parties, laughter. He gave her a silver bracelet in thanks. She'd worn it every day.

He had been her friend, had always treated her with respect. Unlike the others, who snickered at her cheaply made clothes and called her cruel names. At the end, Tom had proven to be just like them. She had run home, her heart broken, and thrown the bracelet in her jewelry box, never to wear it again.

Too bad she couldn't have discarded her heart as easily. But Tom's betrayal had strengthened her, made her more determined to protect herself, to control her own destiny.

"I'm done peeling," he said. "What else can I do?"

She shoved old memories aside. Tom was her boss now, nothing more. And someday he wouldn't even be that.

"Let me have the potatoes," she said, turning to him. "I need to cut them up."

He hugged the bowl. "I won't let you kill these like you did the celery."

She couldn't help laughing. He could always make her laugh.

"Just give me the bowl." She glanced at the clock. "We're running out of time. I wish Gail would get back."

"What am I—chopped liver? I said I'd help." He handed her the bowl. "You're the boss in the kitchen."

The timer on the oven shrilled. She handed him two potholders. "You can take the roast out."

"Sure, Chef," he said, saluting.

Mary Beth rolled her eyes at him and grabbed a potato.

"You do nice work," she said, holding up a perfectly peeled, white orb.

"I aim to please." He set the roast on the stovetop. "Smells great," he said, inhaling deeply. "How about if I take a little chunk." He looked at her, his hand poised over the meat.

"Don't you dare," Mary Beth said, batting his hand away.

He laughed, making her smile.

"I got another smile out of you," he said. "That's good." His intense gaze weakened her defenses. She shifted.

"I have to cut these," she said in a shaky voice. She groped the counter for her knife.

"What's for dessert?" he asked.

"Lemon pound cake. It's in the refrigerator."

He opened the refrigerator and peered in. "Wow! It's a work of art. Hanging around here could be dangerous."

Not as dangerous as being around you. The thought leapt unbidden into Mary Beth's mind. She dropped the potato. It rolled on the floor. She bent to retrieve it.

"I'll get it," Tom said.

Their heads collided. Mary Beth rocked back on her heels and rubbed her forehead. Tom crouched in front of her, concern in his eyes. He reached out and gently stroked her temple.

She swayed toward him, as if her body had a will of its own.

Tom's blue eyes darkened. "Mary Beth," he whispered.

Fear filled her heart . . . fear of losing herself, of weakening. She jumped up.

"I'll–I'll wash this off," she stammered, clutching the vegetable as if it could save her from her response to him.

She hurried to the sink and jerked on the faucet. The force of the water almost knocked the potato from her hand.

Tom cleared his throat. "What else do you need?"

She needed him to leave so she could be in charge of her kitchen again and not be such a bumbling idiot. Mary Beth drew a deep breath. What she really needed was to take charge of her emotions.

"You can fill that with water," she said, nodding toward the stockpot that rested on the counter.

She moved away from the double sink to give him room, not trusting herself so close to him.

The muscles of his forearms flexed as he held the large pot under the faucet. A hard stream of water splashed into the heavy metal. Seeing him cradle the pot in his strong arms made Mary Beth ache. She wanted Tom's arms around her, holding her. She leaned against the counter and closed her eyes, fighting for control.

The citrus of his cologne, so like his high school scent but more subtle and expensive, teased her, provoking memories, and regret.

"Is this enough water?" Tom asked.

She gazed into his deep blue eyes and nodded her head, not trusting herself to speak.

A bemused expression crossed Tom's features. He held the pot up. "Where do you want this?"

"Put it on the right back burner and turn the gas on high." Her voice sounded shaky.

Tom positioned the pot and turned on the heat. Flames licked the bottom of the ironclad pan.

"What next?" He stood directly in front of her.

His beautiful mouth was so close. She could just reach out a finger and. . . .

"You have water on your face," he whispered huskily. He smoothed his thumb gently along her cheekbone. The warmth of his touch melted her resistance.

Need and longing wrapped themselves around her heart.

Part of her screamed to back away, to protect herself. But Tom's masculinity reeled her slowly into his net.

He bent his head toward hers.

"Hey, you two, what's cooking?" Gail's voice boomed from the doorway.

Mary Beth and Tom jumped apart. Mary Beth dropped the potato. It bounced along the floor, landing at Gail's feet.

Chapter Three

"**I** need more money. How do you expect me to live? I have standards to maintain."

Mary Beth winced and clutched the cordless phone as her mother's voice droned on. She could recite Dorothy Kendrick's litany of complaints by heart.

"Mom," she interrupted. "Two weeks ago I gave you enough food money for a month. It can't be gone already."

"I have other expenses. My Green Thumb Ladies Garden Club fees were due."

Clenching her jaw, Mary Beth paced the length of her living room. The floorboards of the old Victorian squeaked the protest she couldn't voice. *Give me strength,* she prayed.

"Mom," she said slowly. "You know money's tight right now. I can barely pay your mortgage and living expenses. The hospital is hounding me about the bills from your surgery last year. There isn't extra for frivolous garden club fees."

"Well . . . If you had taken that job at the bank instead of insisting on running your own business, we wouldn't be in this fix now."

Mary Beth breathed deeply and stared out of the floor-to-ceiling windows at bustling Trolley Square. How many of those pedestrians scurrying by on the street two floors below had a clinging, ungrateful mother who . . . She bit back her unkind thoughts.

"I don't want to be a banker, Mom. I'm a chef. It's what I do. What I'm happiest at."

"Happy?" Dorothy sniffed. "I sacrificed my happiness to put you through that fancy prep school and college."

"I got scholarships, Mom. To all the schools."

"So, I didn't make any sacrifices?"

"I didn't say you didn't make some sacrifices. It's just that things would have been easier had you gotten a job."

Darn! Too late. She should have kept her mouth shut. Flinching, Mary Beth held the phone away from her ear and prepared for the tirade to come.

"My job was to stay home and raise you, and I did that well. Your father's duty was to provide for his family. He shirked his responsibilities, running off with that woman, and gallivanting around the world." Her mother's soft sobs stabbed Mary Beth like an ice pick to the heart.

She collapsed onto the softness of her sofa and grabbed one of the silk throw pillows, pressing it to her stomach as if it could blot out years of humiliation and unhappiness.

Her mother had been screeching this same lament since Mary Beth was eight and Brian Kendrick walked out on them. Her father's betrayal still made her stomach clench and bile rise in her throat.

"I'm sorry, Mom. I know you sacrificed a lot for me. You even taught me to cook." The time spent with her mother in the kitchen had brightened her bleak childhood. Mary Beth blinked away tears. "We're getting on our feet again," she said. "Sackett Industries bought a controlling interest in our company. Things should be better."

"Sackett?" her mother said. "Didn't you have a crush on that wealthy Sackett boy? If you hadn't been so darn stubborn and independent, you could have snagged yourself a rich husband. Someone who could take care of you. And me. Why do you think I sent you to that fancy school?"

Mary Beth squeezed her eyes shut at the bitter accusation in her mother's voice. Tom. He had betrayed her too. Just like her father.

"I can take care of myself, Mom."

"Just like you've taken care of yourself so far," her mother snapped.

Mary Beth counted slowly to ten. "Things will get better. I promise. I just don't have money for extras right now. Why don't you find a little job for a while?

You're good with plants. Mrs. Price has been after you to work in her florist shop."

"I am very good with flowers and greenery." Her mother sniffed.

"Think about it, Mom. I have to go now. I'll try to scrape together some money for you."

Mary Beth hung up the phone and clutched the pillow closer, bunching the smooth fabric in her fist and rocking back and forth. Never, ever would she be like her mother, so dependent on a man that she couldn't function when he left.

An image of Tom pushed into her mind. She had let him get too close the other day in the kitchen. That wouldn't happen again.

Mary Beth transferred warm crabmeat balls and mushrooms stuffed with spinach onto silver servers. Gail handed the platters to the three college students hired to help the regular staff at the Bennett mansion.

"So far everything's going according to plan," Mary Beth said when the students had left with their heavy trays.

"The evening's early yet," Gail said. "Let's keep our fingers crossed."

Mary Beth wiped her hands on a paper towel. "I hope they like the rest of the meal as much as they seem to enjoy the appetizers and caviar."

Gail smiled. "Considering the copious amount of liquor flowing from Jim Bennett's wine cellar, they may not notice the food at all."

"I prefer them sober when they taste this exquisite meal we've slaved over all day," Mary Beth said.

"If you have to slave in a kitchen, this is the place," Gail said.

Mary Beth followed Gail's gaze around the spacious, professionally equipped kitchen with its two commercial refrigerators, four ovens, two dishwashers, and a butler's pantry. The rich walnut cabinets were a sharp contrast to the satiny almond-colored walls and the beige countertops inlaid with antique hand-painted tiles.

"This is quite a house," Mary Beth said. "In all the years I went to school with Taylor Bennett, she never invited me here." She threw Gail a rueful look. "Of course, kids who lived in Chateau Country didn't associate with kids from working-class neighborhoods."

"You're here now and it won't be the last time," Gail said. "Their cook's broken ankle turned out to be our lucky break."

"That's a lame joke," Mary Beth said, smiling. She sighed. "It still grates on me that we were available on such short notice."

Gail shrugged. "Don't worry about it. By this time next year we'll have a waiting list for our services. And this job's bringing a lot of money."

"I could sure use the money," Mary Beth said.

It had been a week since her mother's telephone call. With the substantial fee from the Bennetts, she'd send her a check.

The timer shrilled, propelling her and Gail into action. They removed trays of stuffed mushrooms from one of the wall ovens. Mary Beth inhaled the pungent odor of garlic and chives. At least in the kitchen she could relax, free from worries.

They set the hot trays on ceramic trivets to cool and then removed crabmeat balls from another of the ovens.

"This job is just the beginning for us," Gail said. "See what Tom's connections can do?"

Tom. Mary Beth hadn't seen him in ten days, since he'd helped her prepare the lamb stew. She had liked being with him, liked it too much. He would have kissed her if Gail hadn't interrupted. She should be grateful to Gail. Instead she felt . . . cheated.

Since then her nights had been filled with romantic dreams of kissing Tom and holding him close. Of running her fingers through his thick black hair. She sighed as the memories warmed her like steam from a boiling pot.

Get over it, she told herself. *You're not in high school anymore with a crush on the cutest guy in class.*

She had to push Tom away, had to protect herself from hurt. He'd be here tonight, one of the guests. She would be cool and professional. He'd never know the emotional turmoil his nearness provoked.

The student servers and the Bennett maids entered the kitchen with empty platters. She spent the next minutes refilling trays.

"I've got to start that cream sauce for the lobster ravioli," she said when the others had left.

"I'd better get the salads out of the refrigerator," Gail said.

"Mr. Sackett, that's just the kitchen in that direction." The voice of Frederick, the butler, drifted in from the long hallway.

"I know exactly where I'm going, Freddy." At the sound of Tom's deep voice Mary Beth stopped on her way to the refrigerator and whirled to face the doorway.

"How are my two favorite caterers?" Tom sauntered into the room.

He smiled at Gail before settling his gaze on Mary Beth. The intensity in his eyes held her in place. She tugged on her braid as butterflies whipped a soufflé in her stomach. Why did Tom always have to look so devastatingly handsome? It just wasn't fair.

Tonight he wore a well-cut deep blue suit that accentuated the breadth of his powerful shoulders. His snowy shirt and exquisite silk tie complemented the picture of moneyed elegance. Only his black hair, softly curling over his collar, hinted at the wild youth he'd once been.

Mary Beth rubbed her hands down the sides of her linen slacks, wishing that just once Tom could see her dressed in something other than plain black pants and a white blouse.

She breathed deeply. She was Tom's employee. Nothing more. How she looked didn't matter.

"The appetizers are a hit," he said. "I can't wait to taste the rest of the dinner." He didn't move his gaze from Mary Beth.

"I've got some things in the butler's pantry I have to check," Gail said, heading for the small room off the kitchen.

"You look nice," Tom said when they were alone.

His warm smile made the butterflies in her stomach churn out of control.

"The Bennetts were thoughtful enough to provide us a room to shower and change," Mary Beth said.

He studied her. "You've been avoiding me, Mary Beth." He walked slowly toward her. The subtle scent of his cologne teased her with sweet memories. "You wouldn't take any of my telephone calls the past week," he continued.

"Gail can handle the business as well as I can," she said, backing away from him. "And business is the only thing between you and me."

His jaw tightened. "I know that, but I wanted to talk to you." His gaze softened. "I enjoyed myself that day in your kitchen."

She twisted her braid around her hand. Just looking at him made her bones liquefy. She lifted her chin. He had betrayed her trust and hurt her deeply once. She had to remember that.

"I have a cream sauce to prepare." She yanked open the refrigerator door and pulled out light cream, butter, and several large shallots.

"Don't run away from me, Mary Beth. We have to talk."

She deposited her armload of ingredients on the counter and wiped her hands on her apron before turning to face him. Their eyes locked. Her chest ached with yearning. She balled her hands into fists. She had to be strong.

"Now's not the time," she said. "And besides, we have nothing to discuss."

He ran his hand over his hair. "We have plenty to say."

She blew her breath out. "I appreciate everything you've done for us. You got us this job, which is a tremendous opportunity. You're my boss. Let's leave it at that."

He stood just inches from her. She stared at his chiseled lips, at the light shadowing of beard on his face. She wanted to trace her finger over his mouth and the firm line of his jaw. She bit down on her lip, forcing the dangerous thoughts from her mind.

"I'm not your boss, Mary Beth," he said. Frustration edged his voice. "Kendrick's is a subsidiary of Sackett. You and I were friends once."

"We're business associates now," she said, angling her chin. "Nothing more."

"Is that the way you want it?" he asked.

"That's the way I want it." *Liar,* a small voice taunted.

He moved away. Sadness coiled around her heart.

"Tom, darling, there you are." A soft, melodious voice came from the doorway. Mary Beth shuddered.

Taylor Bennett, six foot two inches in her stiletto heels, her silver blond hair in an elegant French twist, slithered into the kitchen. Her black silk sheath skimmed the rich curves of her long body. Diamonds twinkled from her delicate earlobes.

Taylor latched onto Tom's arm, clinging to him like glazed caramel on crème brûlée.

Mary Beth moved away, glad to put distance between herself and the privileged couple who matched each other in height and breeding.

Old hurts twisted in her like a serrated knife. She was back in high school, the poor kid on scholarship surrounded by the children of the elite. She straightened her spine. She'd worked hard and made something of herself. No one could take that away from her.

Tom stepped away from Taylor. The blond's full red lips formed a pout. "If I didn't know better, I'd think you were avoiding me, Tom. Last night you left the Edwards's party early, and now I find you in the kitchen with the help." Her cold, pale blue gaze slid over Mary Beth.

Tom narrowed his eyes at Taylor. "Mary Beth is a professional chef," he said. "And a darn good one. She came to your mother's rescue."

"Mary Beth Kendrick." Taylor's lip curled in a sneer. "You haven't grown at all since school. You still look like a little girl."

Mary Beth's face heated. "Hello, Taylor. It's been a long time. I can't say you look eighteen anymore. Every one of the past twelve years is. . . ."

"Hi, I'm Gail O'Connell, Mary Beth's partner. We haven't met." Taylor ignored Gail's outstretched hand.

Mary Beth threw Gail a look. Gail shrugged.

Tom glanced at Mary Beth. His mouth tilted into a smile that he quickly suppressed. "Taylor, we should leave and let these ladies get back to the work they do so well."

Taylor twined her arm through his. The blood red of her long lacquered nails stood out against the dark blue of his jacket, like talons imprisoning their prey.

"Come on, Tommy." She flicked her icy gaze at Mary Beth and ran her hand slowly up Tom's arm. "The conversation in the drawing room is much more stimulating. And Daddy just opened a bottle of his best Sauvignon Blanc."

"Go on ahead," he said, pulling his arm free of hers. "We have some business to discuss here. I'll join you shortly."

With a toss of her head, Taylor pranced from the room.

"We need to talk, Mary Beth," Tom said. His gaze caught hers.

"We're finished talking," she said. "I have a dinner to cook."

A muscle worked in his jaw. "Later," he said. He strode from the room.

The excitement and tension that surrounded Mary

Beth whenever Tom was near left with him. She felt deflated, like a pie cut too soon.

"What was that all about?" Gail asked.

"Nothing," Mary Beth said.

"That Taylor's something else," Gail said. "A real spoiled b . . . brat. Tom didn't seem to appreciate her charms."

"They're old friends," Mary Beth said. "They dated in school." Remembered hurt made her stomach turn. She pushed the old memories aside. "We have work to do," she said. "By the way, thanks for bailing me out." She threw Gail a pointed look. "I almost rose to Taylor's bait. If you hadn't broken in when you did, God knows what I would have said."

Gail laughed. "When I heard her say you looked like a little girl, I knew we were in trouble. I tripped all over myself getting in here."

"I know I have to bite my tongue at times for the sake of the business," Mary Beth said. "But what satisfaction I would have gotten telling Taylor Bennett exactly what I think of her."

Mary Beth sipped ice water and leaned against the butcher-block island in the Bennett kitchen.

Gail sat on a stool opposite her. Perspiration beaded her forehead and she pushed blond curls off her face.

"We did it," Mary Beth said, raising her glass in salute. She and Gail were alone in the quiet kitchen while the staff served desserts and coffee.

"And did it well," Gail said. She nodded toward the

doorway. "Sounds like they're enjoying their desserts as much as they did the rest of the meal."

Laughter and the delicate musical tinkling of sterling flatware on bone china came from the huge dining room where two massive tables seated all thirty of the Bennetts' guests.

Mary Beth set her glass on the island and rubbed her arms. Her muscles ached from cooking and from hauling heavy pots. But it was all worth it.

She surveyed the kitchen and its counters littered with dirty plates, glasses, and serving pieces. No leftovers in sight. All signs of a well-enjoyed meal.

The staff would clean up later. She and Gail had already washed their personal knives, the only equipment they'd needed to bring. Once they got the Bennetts' check they'd be on their way.

"Did you see Jim Bennett's eyes when we brought out the rum-glazed pears?" Gail asked.

Mary Beth grinned. "I thought they'd pop right out of his head, especially when you topped the pears with whipped cream."

"How about the professor-type guy with the ascot," Gail said, laughing. "He looked ready to lunge over the table for the sponge cake."

"It's a wonder they had room for dessert the way they wolfed down our Saltimbocca alla Romana and risotto." Mary Beth kissed her fingertips and threw the kiss into the room. "The best we've ever made."

"Darn, we're good," Gail said. "Slap me five."

Laughing, Mary Beth exchanged high fives with Gail.

"Can you believe we actually got a standing ovation?" Mary Beth asked.

"A standing ovation from everyone except Taylor." Gail grimaced.

"We don't need Taylor." Mary Beth waved her hand in dismissal. "After tonight our reputation in this town is sealed."

"And we spread our business cards around like pâté on crackers," Gail said. "Our phone will start ringing off the hook."

Mary Beth finished her water and rolled the icy glass over her forehead. She focused on the copper pots hanging on a wall grid. "We can buy our business back and I won't need Tom anymore," she whispered.

"Maybe you'll need him in other ways," Gail said softly.

Realizing Gail had heard her, Mary Beth's face burned. "What are you talking about?"

Gail arched an eyebrow. "He couldn't stop looking at you every time you went into the dining room."

Mary Beth stiffened. "He wasn't looking at me."

"You noticed," Gail said.

Not wanting to meet Gail's knowing gaze, Mary Beth glanced away. She knew Tom watched her. She had tried to ignore him, but she couldn't help sliding looks his way. Her pulse had raced every time their gazes connected. She couldn't tell Gail that, and hated admitting it to herself.

"Then of course there was Taylor," Gail said. "You must have felt the sting of her venom stares."

"I felt nothing," Mary Beth said in a tight voice. "Subject closed."

An hour later, check in hand, Mary Beth clutched her knife case, ready to leave the rarefied world of the Bennetts. The staff bustled around cleaning counters and loading dishwashers. Gail was on the phone to Pete.

Mary Beth scanned the large room and sighed. Their night had been a raging success. Maybe soon she'd be free to run her own business, free of Tom and the heady, disturbing emotions he invoked in her.

Her chest ached. Tom would be gone from her life. No problem. She'd done very well without him the past twelve years.

"Ready to go?" Gail said, coming to her side.

"Ready," Mary Beth said. She glanced at the doorway. Its emptiness mocked her. No Tom leaning against the frame, smiling. Why would he care when they left? They were no more than employees to him. She blinked her eyes against the sudden hurt that blindsided her.

They said their farewells to the staff and started for the side door. Their van was parked at the top of the drive, behind high hedges.

"Leaving without saying good-bye?"

Mary Beth's heart somersaulted. She turned slowly around.

He sauntered toward them, jacketless, his tie loose.

His gaze never wavered from hers, his crooked grin warming her.

"I'll walk you to the car," he said.

"Oh, darn, I have to go to the powder room before we leave," Gail said. "I'll meet you at the van."

No, Mary Beth's mind screamed. *Don't leave me alone with him. I don't trust myself.*

Tom held the door open and she had no choice but to walk out with him into the pine-scented night. She threw her head back to stare at the clear dark sky. Stars were strung across it like a delicate diamond necklace.

An evening made for love, with a dollop of romance. Shivers of fear and excitement skittered up her spine. The safety of the beige catering van beckoned. She hurried her steps.

The van's door rattled in protest as she slid it open and deposited her knife case. Tom stood close behind her. The warmth of his body seemed to vibrate, warning of danger.

She turned to face him. "Thanks for everything," she said. The subtle scent of his cologne drew out sweet memories, making her tremble. She focused on the white blossoms of a nearby rhododendron, trying to ignore the way his nearness made her want to melt into him like honey on a warm biscuit.

"I only got you the job," he said softly. "You made it a success."

She felt him looking at her, but she refused to meet his gaze.

He touched her shoulder. She tensed.

"Look at me, Cat Eyes," he said huskily.

"Cat Eyes?" She stared up at him.

"Darn," he said, skimming his hand over his hair. "It's just my secret name for you."

"Don't have a secret name for me, Tom." She clenched her jaw.

He reached out a hand and tucked a wayward curl behind her ear.

Gasping, she touched her ear. It burned from his caress.

"In all the time I've known you, I've never seen your hair free," he said in a thick voice.

She looked into his eyes, dark and mysterious in the moonlight, and knew that she was lost.

"You are so beautiful," he said, stroking her jaw with his thumb.

Her body pulsed with dreams that had gone unrealized in all the years since high school. She had to fight her weakness, but the night was so sweet and warm and Tom was so close.

He bent toward her.

"What are you doing?" she said in a shaky voice.

"Fulfilling a fantasy," he whispered.

He pulled her to him. His lips, hot and soft, crushed hers. He tasted of hazelnut coffee and whipped cream. Time seemed to stop; her fears no longer existed. Nothing mattered but this moment and this man. She wrapped her arms around his neck.

"Mary Beth," he whispered against her mouth. The

longing in his voice awakened an answering need in her.

"Tommy, Tommy, are you out here?" Taylor's voice hit Mary Beth with the force of a cast-iron pot.

She jerked away. Tears stung her eyes. She didn't belong in Tom's world, not then, not now.

"I won't be your fantasy, Tom."

"Mary Beth." The pain in his voice shot through her. She stiffened. He'd used her once. No more.

"Go," she said, backing up against the van.

Hurt shadowed his face. He reached out a finger and gently traced her lips before turning and walking slowly away.

A single tear slipped down her cheek.

Chapter Four

Kissing Mary Beth last night had been stupid. He'd been out of line to force himself on her. But he hadn't forced himself, had he?

Tom eased his car into the parking space on the tree-lined street and cut the engine. He leaned back against the soft leather seat. His head pounded like bumper cars taking a test drive.

Laughter erupted from the nearby sidewalk café and he glanced over. He wished he could enjoy the Sunday afternoon sunshine like the restaurant patrons and the couples who strolled languidly along the quiet walkways of Trolley Square.

Thoughts of Mary Beth drove peace from his mind. Her pride and beauty, the warmth of her kiss, stirred him. She'd enjoyed kissing him—he hadn't imagined that.

He yanked the keys from the ignition and clenched his hand around the hard metal. He needed her friendship and forgiveness. He'd never earn either if he couldn't keep his hands to himself.

Easier said than done. Every time he saw Mary Beth he wanted to kiss her and hold her.

The closeness they'd shared that day when he helped her cook, the awareness that always swirled around them, had made him want to spend time with her, to know the woman she'd become. Apparently she hadn't felt the same way about him. She'd ignored him after that, not even taking his calls. Her coolness last night at the Bennett party frustrated him further. He had needed to touch her, to have her smile just for him.

Had he really thought she'd be so grateful he had bailed out her business that she'd forgive him everything and fall willingly into his arms?

No worshipful acquiescence from Mary Beth. With other women he merely had to smile and they came running. Not his Cat Eyes. Never.

Her stubbornness and pride twisted his mouth into a reluctant grin. He'd always admired those traits in her, but not when they were directed against him.

He'd dated plenty of women over the years, but no one, not even Clarice, could make him forget Mary Beth. He refused to question why.

Stop it, he told himself. He had to quit obsessing over her.

He jerked open the car door and slid out, banging

the door shut so hard that the windows rattled. He'd been thinking too much lately.

He'd apologize to her and leave. His assistant could handle any business transactions involving Kendrick and Company. There'd be no reason to see her except at occasional corporate functions. Regret slapped at him, but he shoved it aside.

Taking a deep breath, he walked up the steps of the brightly colored Victorian and rang the bell for the second floor.

"Who is it?" Her voice, low and breathy, came through the speaker. His chest constricted.

"Tom." He winced at the answering huskiness in his tone. "Can I come up?" Silence. Anxiety gnawed at him. Maybe she wouldn't see him. The outside door unlocked with a click. He released his breath.

His heart thumping like a sixteen-year-old with his first crush, Tom took the steps two at a time.

Mary Beth stood in the open doorway at the top of the stairs, outlined against the sunlight that streamed into the room behind her. She looked like Venus rising from the sea. Her glorious mane of red-gold hair curled freely around her face and over her shoulders, just as he'd always imagined. The T-shirt and cut-off jeans she wore showed the perfection of her shapely body.

Her beauty stole his breath, and his heart. He approached her almost reverently.

"Your hair is loose," he said. He could only stare.

Her high cheekbones turned pink. "What do you want?" she said in a thick voice.

He wanted to gather her in his arms and tangle his hands in the silky strands of her burnished hair. His words of apology turned to dust in his mouth.

"I came to apologize for kissing you last night, but I can't do that now. I still want to kiss you."

Her color heightened and her bottom lip trembled. She turned away.

He grabbed her arm and pulled her gently around to face him. Her skin was soft, warm. She smelled like spring lilacs.

"You'd better go," she said, her voice shaky. She freed her arm from his grip and walked into her apartment.

He followed, closing the door behind him.

She turned. "I told you to leave," she said. Tight lines formed around her mouth.

He leaned against the door. A ginger-colored cat walked over to him and rubbed against his leg. He bent to stroke its silky fur. It purred loudly. If only Mary Beth would purr at his touch.

"I don't regret kissing you," he said, straightening. "I've wanted to do that since the first day I saw you again. You are a beautiful and special woman."

Surprised pleasure touched her eyes before a mask dropped over her features. She folded her arms across her chest, stubbornness in every curve of her body. "Don't, Tom. We're business associates. Period. It grates on me that I had to accept your help, but I respect what you've done for my company. You may own Kendrick's now, but you don't own me. I'm not your plaything."

He flinched. "Plaything? My God, I never thought of you like that, ever."

Green fire flashed from her eyes. "You never thought of me like that? I remember a night when you threw me to your friends like I was some little toy for their amusement."

He raked his fingers through his hair, frustrated. "I was eighteen. Sit down. We'll get this out of our systems so we can both go on with our lives."

He moved toward her. She backed away to stand by the large windows.

"We have nothing to discuss," she said, lifting her chin in proud defiance.

He closed the distance between them. She held her ground. The hard line of her jaw and the faint glimmer of unshed tears stabbed him with twin blades of anger and guilt.

"We were kids, Mary Beth. I was a coward. I'm not proud of it, but it's over."

"Is that what you call it . . . cowardice?" she said, her voice low. "I call it betrayal, a premeditated cruel act."

"No," he said, reaching out to touch her arm. "It wasn't like that."

She moved away, her hands at her sides. "If you want absolution, go to confession." She pushed aside a sheer lace curtain to stare out the window.

"You're so darn stubborn," he said. "Let it go."

"There is nothing to let go." A pulse throbbed in her neck. "I learned a valuable lesson that night. Even people I think are friends will use and hurt me. You taught me well, Tom."

He winced. "You despise me. More than I thought."

She looked at him. The hurt in her exquisite emerald eyes sliced through his heart.

"Your betrayal made me strong. I'm proud of what I have accomplished. On my own. I should thank you for that." A short bitter laugh escaped her.

Anger and frustration twisted his gut. He clenched his hands to keep from touching her. He wanted to shake some sense into her. He wanted to kiss her until the past dissolved and she melted in his arms.

"Mary Beth."

She held her hand up, silencing him. "All I care about now is saving my business. I'll work with you on that, but anything else between us died a long time ago. Dredging it up serves no purpose. Leave it alone."

"I can't leave it, or you, alone," he whispered. He captured one of her long silky curls and twirled it slowly around his finger.

Her eyes softened. A glimmer of hope opened in his heart. She didn't completely loathe him.

"Leave," she said, pulling away. She brushed her hair back from her face with a shaking hand.

"I'm ready to talk whenever you are," he said. He placed a light kiss on her trembling lips.

Regret and determination stiffened his spine as he

turned and strode quickly out of her apartment, closing the door behind him.

Firm resolve quickened his steps and he ran down the stairs, his jaw tight. He slammed the outside door. Business associates. He'd change her mind about that.

Mary Beth started at the sound of the door slamming. Tears burned her eyes, but she refused to let them fall. She sank into the sofa. Her cat jumped onto her lap and stared up at her. The animal's big green eyes seemed to ask a question. A question Mary Beth couldn't answer.

"Oh, Missy," she said, grabbing the bundle of fur close. "What a fool I am."

She shouldn't have let Tom into her apartment today. Into her life. It hurt to look at him, to be near him. He was so beautiful, with his deep blue eyes framed by thick black lashes, his chiseled features and strong jaw. She found his inborn confidence, mixed with a dash of arrogance, appealing. Too appealing. She had loved him so much once.

Despite everything, the pain, the fears, she'd wanted to kiss him last night. Wanted to kiss him today.

No! She grabbed one of the small pillows from the sofa and threw it across the room, venting her frustration. Missy meowed her protest and jumped from her arms.

Mary Beth tucked a stray curl behind her ear. The memory of Tom touching her hair, longing in his eyes, swept over her, warming her.

She squeezed her eyes shut. She would never let

herself forget the lessons of the past. To let go would weaken her. If she didn't allow anyone into her heart, she would never be hurt again.

Her life had been plotted out so carefully. She'd been so focused on her career, on proving to the world, to herself, that she, Mary Beth Kendrick, needed no man. Then Tom had showed up again. And things would never be the same. She bit her lip, tasting salty tears.

Mary Beth entered the empty reception area of Kendrick and Company and hung her handbag on the closet hook. It was just past 4:30 and Mrs. Hagerty had left for the day.

The sound of Gail's whistling came from the other room.

"You're awfully cheerful," Mary Beth said, going into the kitchen.

Gail looked up from kneading bread dough. "Someone around here has to be happy. You've been Ms. Grumpy for the last three days."

"I have a lot on my mind." Mary Beth opened the refrigerator, pulled out a pitcher of lemonade, and poured herself a glass.

Gail raised an eyebrow. "Care to talk about it?"

"It's nothing." Mary Beth took a sip of lemonade. "Sure is hot for this time of year." She slid her gaze from Gail's.

She'd never told Gail about Tom's visit to her apartment three days ago, although she'd hardly been able to think of anything else.

Since then she hadn't seen or heard from him. Maybe he had finally accepted that things should remain strictly business between them. A man like Tom must have plenty of women in his life. He didn't need to pursue her. A sliver of sadness cut through her heart.

"You look nice," Gail said. "Very stylish. You'll wow them tonight at the Greek Festival."

Mary Beth shrugged. "Thanks, but I'm not out to wow anyone. I wanted to wear something feminine for a change. I get a little tired of black pants and a white shirt."

"I know what you mean," Gail said.

Mary Beth rubbed her palm down the smooth silk of her print skirt. The delicate ankle-grazing skirt, silk tank top, and strappy high-heeled sandals cost half a month's salary. She didn't care. She wanted to look good.

Maybe her subconscious was telling her she needed to meet a man, someone who would make her forget Tom. She sipped the cool drink and stared at the shaft of late afternoon sunlight illuminating the white tile counter.

The light bouncing off the countertop seemed to reach into her soul, opening the secret place where she kept the truth. There wasn't a man alive who could make her forget Tom Sackett.

Fear cramped her stomach and she gripped the lemonade glass. Tom had shown his true colors years ago. She had to remember that.

"Why so quiet?" Gail asked.

"Just relaxing before facing the crowds at the festival," Mary Beth said. "I wish you'd reconsider and go. I hate going alone."

Gail continued molding the dough, not looking up. "Maybe it won't be so bad," she said. "You never know who you might see." Splashes of color rose in her cheeks.

The doorbell buzzed before she could question Gail. "I'll get it," Mary Beth said, walking into the reception area.

Pulling aside the pleated shade covering the glass-fronted door, she peered out. Tom stood outside. He smiled at her, a hesitant smile that made her heart flip like a Sunday morning pancake.

She unlocked the door and opened it slowly to let him in. "Gail's in the kitchen," she said, sliding her gaze from his. "I'm on my way out."

"I know," he said softly. "I'm going with you."

"What?" she squeaked, jerking her attention back to him.

"I came by earlier." The intensity in his eyes held her. "Gail mentioned you were going to the Greek Festival to sample the food, but that you didn't like going alone. I offered to take you. Didn't she tell you?"

"No, she didn't." Mary Beth glanced toward the

kitchen and narrowed her eyes. That mop-haired blond had gone too far this time.

She took a deep breath and faced him. "No. Absolutely not. I won't go with you. This has been a huge misunderstanding."

"What are you afraid of, Mary Beth?"

The challenge in his eyes stopped her. She strode quickly to the desk and leaned against it, putting distance between her and the utterly delicious man who was relaxing so insolently by the door.

"I am not afraid of anything," she said, tightening her jaw. "I've changed my mind. I'm not going after all."

He walked slowly toward her, his blue eyes like fire, warming her. She pressed against the desk.

Despite her fears, Tom's wild good looks shot darts of excitement up her spine. His midnight hair, slightly damp and slicked back, gave him an aura of edgy sophistication. The pale blue of his golf shirt emphasized the deep color of his eyes.

He took her chin between his fingers and tilted her face toward his. "I don't believe you. I think you're scared I'll tell you how beautiful you look." His silky voice caressed her.

He stroked his thumb along her jaw. She wanted to pull away, but his mesmerizing gaze held her.

His clean-shaven face invited her touch. She inhaled the rainwater scent of his soap.

"I am not going with you," she whispered, with the last crumbs of willpower left in her.

He released her and drew in a ragged breath. "You want just business between us, then that's what it will be. Consider this a business trip. You can handle that, can't you?"

"I can handle anything," she said, raising her chin. "But I still won't go with you."

"Afraid to be alone with me?" he asked, taunting her. The huskiness in his voice set off tiny alarms in her mind. He stood with his arms folded, his expression daring her to answer.

"You're no threat to me," she said with a short laugh.

"Prove it." He moved closer until inches separated them.

She met the challenge in his eyes. "I'll get my purse."

Chapter Five

The grounds of the Greek church had been transformed into an open-air feeding frenzy. Long queues snaked toward food stands selling gyro pitas, grilled lamb, and gooey, mouth-watering pastries. The pungent odors of onion, garlic, and rosemary mingled with sweet honey, promising culinary delights.

Mary Beth inhaled deeply and tried to concentrate on the seductive aromas of the food and not the vibrant, disturbing man walking so close beside her.

The surging crowd pushed her against Tom. He reached out a hand to steady her. She stiffened and pulled away.

"Relax, Mary Beth. You're so uptight it's a wonder you don't shatter. I won't bite." His voice held an icy edge.

She stole a glance over at him. He stared straight ahead, his jaw set in a hard line.

The ride to the festival had been strained, with neither of them saying much. Tension had simmered in the close confines of Tom's luxurious sports car. Had she hurt him by her reluctance to attend the festival with him? Despite what he had done in the past, she had no desire to hurt him. But she had to protect herself.

Tom's cool detachment in the car and now, winding though the smiling, boisterous crowd, scraped her already sharpened nerves.

She slid her attention to him again. The rigid set of his shoulders and the pulse that throbbed in his neck hinted at dark fires held back by a strong will. She shuddered.

"You can't be cold," he said, looking down at her.

She shook her head. "I just caught a breeze."

"Come closer," he said. "I'll warm you." He put his arm around her shoulders and pulled her to him. The feel of his hand on her bare skin sent ripples of heat through her. She knew she should draw away, but he felt so good. And she was tired of fighting her attraction to him. She'd allow herself to relax, for just a little while.

"Let's eat indoors," he said, jerking his head toward the yellow brick building attached to the small, stately church. "It might be less crowded there."

They moved down a walkway lined with booths

selling T-shirts and ornate Greek jewelry. Loud squealing came from the children's amusement rides on the other side of the church.

Tom slid his arm down to her waist, guiding her through the masses pouring in and out of the hall where the dinners were served.

He kept his arm around her even after they'd stopped to survey the milling groups who filled the building. The thin barrier of her silk tank top was no protection against the warmth of his touch. Did he realize his closeness made it hard for her to breathe? To think straight?

She glanced at him, but he was preoccupied, scanning the crowd. She let her breath out. Her imagination was definitely boiling over.

"So much for being less crowded," Tom said, looking at her.

"At least it's more of a controlled chaos," she said, hoping she sounded cool. She couldn't let him know that his nearness had her tied in knots.

"Looks like a long wait," he said, steering her to the end of the food line. The line wound from the lower level, where the meals were served, up the stairs. A railing ran along the upper floor, allowing them to look down at the diners.

But Mary Beth's attention was on Tom. Her gaze drank in his achingly handsome face and full lips. Memories of his kiss, of moonlight and pines, stirred her. She would need all her strength to get through this night with her pride, and her heart, intact.

He caught her staring. Their gazes locked. Blue sparks lit his eyes, drawing her under his spell like a moth seduced by the killing flame. Her cheeks burned.

He cleared his throat. "How about something to drink?"

"Sure," she said in a breathy voice she barely recognized.

He smiled. "Iced tea okay?"

"Iced tea is good," she said.

"I'll get the drinks," he said.

He walked down the stairs with an easy grace, his movements fluid. The muscles of his broad back rippled under his shirt. Her mouth went dry as her gaze followed him.

She clenched her hands into fists. There could never be anything between her and Tom. Too many years and too much hurt stood in the way. She had given him her heart once and he'd thrown it back at her. She wouldn't trust him again.

Tom carefully made his way back up the stairs, carrying two large glasses. The slight smile he gave her reminded her of the young Tom. A sad yearning clutched her. She missed their friendship, the easy camaraderie they'd once shared. She clenched her jaw against this latest assault on her emotional well-being.

He handed her one of the frosted glasses.

She took the drink from him and sipped it, staring at him over the rim of the glass.

A lock of black hair had fallen over his forehead.

Her fingers itched to stroke it back, to touch the silky-looking strands.

With one large gulp, she finished the tea. The cold liquid raced down to her empty stomach, taking her breath away.

"Wow, you must have been thirsty," he said.

Embarrassment heated her and she looked quickly away.

"Mary Beth?" He touched her shoulder, drawing her attention back to him. She looked into cobalt eyes that held uncertainty and challenge.

A muscle worked in his jaw. "I know you didn't want to come here with me. You've hardly said two words since we got in the car. You make me feel like I'm some crumb you can't wait to brush off the table."

He looked so sincere. She put her hand on his arm. "I don't mean to do that to you." She licked her dry lips. "It's just that I'm nervous." She couldn't tell him the truth . . . that she was more afraid of her own growing feelings for him than she was of him.

His smile dissolved her control. "Forget it," he said. "Let's just enjoy the evening. And the food. Even business associates can have fun together. Right?"

She fingered her braid, mustering up her courage. It wouldn't hurt to loosen up a bit. She was a big girl. She could handle Tom and her own swirling emotions. "Let's just concentrate on enjoying this sumptuous-looking food," she said, throwing him a hesitant smile.

His gaze softened. "I always was a sucker for your smile."

Excitement, mixed with a dash of fear, made her heart skip a beat. She glanced away to study the poster-sized menu hanging on the wall.

Fifteen minutes later, laden with heavy trays, she and Tom wound their way between the large, crowded tables. The rich aromas of piquant grape leaves, sweet pastitsio, and spicy moussaka wafted up from her tray, making her stomach rumble in anticipation.

They set their trays on the red-checked cloth of a table occupied by a family of four who were preparing to leave. The young parents smiled at them before herding their restless children out of the noisy dining hall.

"Do you want another tea?" Tom asked.

She nodded.

"Drink this one a littler slower, okay?" he said with a grin.

He reminded her of the young, carefree Tom she once knew, the boy who always made her laugh. She returned his grin.

He winked at her. "I'll get the drinks," he said.

When he'd gone, she attacked the grape leaves, cutting into the succulent dark green vegetable and ground meat as if she could cut Tom and his disturbing presence out of her life.

But she didn't want to cut him out of her life, at least not for tonight. She would forget her fears and allow herself to have fun for a change. It had been such a long time since she'd had any fun.

Tom returned and set a large glass of iced tea in

front of her and another one near his plate. "Everything looks and smells so good," he said, pulling a chair close to her and sitting down.

Mary Beth cut another chunk of food and popped it into her mouth. Keep eating, she told herself. If she kept busy she wouldn't notice how close Tom sat, how his clean scent of soap with a hint of cologne tantalized her more than the food on her plate.

"These dolmades are so good," she said. *Concentrate on the food. That's why you're here.* Chewing slowly, she savored the tart-sweet taste, trying to identify the myriad of spices and that one special ingredient unique to each serious cook.

"Dolmades?" Tom said. "You mean the stuffed grape leaves? My favorite is this macaroni, cheese, and hamburger stuff."

Mary Beth laughed. "That 'stuff' as you call it is pastitsio. And it's got a whole lot more going for it than macaroni, cheese, and hamburger."

Tom shrugged. "Hey, what do I know? I'm just a simple, unsophisticated guy."

"I doubt that," she said, raising an eyebrow. "You lived in New York City for years, didn't you?"

"Just a few." He slid another forkful of pastitsio into his mouth.

She watched him chew, fascinated by the movement of his jaw muscles. Wrapping her hand around her glass, she fought to keep from touching the smooth column of his throat.

"You were in New York more than a few years,"

she said. "I heard you went to law school at Columbia, then lived and worked in Manhattan until recently."

"Have you been keeping tabs on me, Mary Beth?" he asked softly. The intensity of his gaze made her quickly look away.

"Wilmington's a small place. People talk." She sipped some tea.

"So what do people say about me?"

"Just that you worked for some fancy law firm on Wall Street." She stabbed the last of the grape leaves with her fork and slipped the food into her mouth. A full mouth would keep her from babbling.

"I practiced law in New York. That part is right." Pain flickered in Tom's eyes before he glanced away.

Jealousy cut through Mary Beth with the swiftness of a knife. Did Tom leave behind a woman in New York? Did he love the woman so much that just talking about the city caused him pain?

Pushing the dangerous thoughts out of her mind, Mary Beth speared a piece of moussaka. She pushed the food around on her plate, studying the layers of ground lamb, eggplant, and potatoes. Tom's love life, past or present, did not concern her in the least.

"The New York part of my life is over," he said. He took a long sip of his drink. His gaze seemed to settle on a spot above her head. "I had to come back to Wilmington to finish some unsettled business." He shifted in his chair and looked at her. "My family needed me too."

"Your family?" she said.

"Mom and Dad are getting up in years. Dad hasn't been the same since the accident. They want to retire. My sister and her husband pretty much run the company, but Maureen is pregnant with her third and she'd like to spend more time at home. They've been after me for years to take my place at the company. I decided it was time to come home."

"They say you can't go home again," she said quietly.

"They may be right," he said. "I'll find out." His gaze locked with hers. He looked vulnerable and unsure of himself. She wanted to glide her fingers over his proud features, to assure him he'd made the right decision. The truth nudged her. She wanted more than that, but it was just business between them. She could never allow anything else. Sadness pinched at her insides.

Around them children screamed and babies cried. Laughter and loud talk bubbled from nearby tables. Mary Beth barely noticed. She saw only Tom.

"Mary Beth," Tom said, a question in his voice. He moved closer. Her breath caught. He leaned toward her.

"I'm glad I came home," he said quietly.

"Are you?" she whispered. She almost believed him.

"Yes." He touched the corner of her mouth with his thumb. His cobalt gaze caught hers in a spell she couldn't break.

"Mind if we sit here?"

Mary Beth blinked and jumped back, away from Tom and temptation.

An elderly couple, holding trays overflowing with food, smiled down at them.

"Please sit," Tom said.

Mary Beth picked up her fork and began cutting the pastitsio. She forced the tension from her muscles. She had to get a grip on her vivid imagination.

The elderly couple sat across from them. The woman smiled and laid her hand over the man's on the table. "You two look like nice young people," she said. "Frank and I have been married fifty years. We wish you the same happiness together we've had."

"We're not a couple," Mary Beth said. "We're just business associates." *Business, business, business,* she repeated like a mantra, trying to carve it into her brain.

"That's some business," the man said, raising his eyebrows.

"She is a bit of a workaholic," Tom said, patting Mary Beth's hand.

She kicked him under the table.

"Ow." He winced. The older couple stared at them.

"Enjoy your meal," Tom said. "Don't let us disturb you."

"Workaholic," Mary Beth muttered. "Very funny."

"I love it when your eyes flash like that," he said. "Speaking of eyes, did you know that the green of that very becoming top you're wearing exactly matches your eyes?"

"Stop it right now," she said. "We're here to check out the food for my—our company, remember?"

"Okay," he said, leaning back. "You want to talk shop, let's talk. How did you get into catering?" The intimate tone of his voice and his probing gaze gave the question a decidedly unprofessional slant.

"You don't look like you want to discuss business." She took a mouthful of pastitsio.

His lips tilted into a teasing grin. "Catering is your career, isn't it?" His gaze dropped to her mouth. "But I'll discuss any subject you want," he said softly.

She tossed back the last of her tea and moved her chair away from his, trying to ignore the way her stomach churned at the glint in his blue eyes. Catering was a nice safe topic. She'd stick to that. "I majored in biology in school," she said, "but I've always loved to cook. I made meals for my college roommates and catered the parties we threw. I decided I wanted to make cooking my life's work."

"What are your long-range plans? Professionally speaking, of course," Tom said.

She drew herself up and met his gaze. "Gail and I hope to open a small restaurant some day. Something exclusive where we can serve unique dishes." Voicing her dream made her swell with pride.

He frowned. "A good goal, but it'll take lots of work, and most new restaurants don't make it."

She tensed. "We know that, but we're not afraid of hard work and we have faith in ourselves."

"I have faith in you too," he said, smiling. "I didn't mean to suggest otherwise."

She glanced away. It was hard to remember that he'd broken her heart once when he was being so nice and attentive now. Her emotions wouldn't be taking such a pummeling if Tom were cold and arrogant.

Mary Beth looked at the elderly couple. They beamed at her. She managed a weak smile.

"Mary Beth?" Tom said, grabbing her attention.

She faced him. Darn, his eyes were so blue. It just wasn't fair.

"Did you cook when we were in high school?" he asked.

She nodded.

"You never invited me to your house for dinner," he said.

"Invite you to my house, Tom? Get real. You lived in Chateau Country. I lived in a broken down apartment in Claymont."

"I didn't care about that stuff. I would have come if you'd asked me."

She stared down at the table. The red and white checks of the tablecloth swam before her eyes. If he hadn't cared about their differences, why did he set her up at the formal? She swallowed around the lump in her throat.

"Let's go," she said, standing. "I've eaten enough." She glanced at the food left on her plate. Normally she scarfed these delicacies up, but being with Tom put her nerves on edge and dulled her appetite.

Holding small plastic containers of assorted pastries, they walked out of the church hall into a dusky blue twilight teeming with festivalgoers. Heady, throbbing Greek music came from the stage set up in a corner of the church parking lot.

"Let's see if we can get a table and listen to the music," Tom said. "Is that all right with you?" His lopsided grin made her heart kick like one of the Greek dancers on the stage.

"I'll take you home if you want," he said, "but it's kind of early to call it a night. And we still have these pastries to eat. I promised Gail a report on the desserts."

A light breeze, like a ghostly omen, whispered across Mary Beth's skin. She looked up at the first stars of the night, translucent diamonds thrown on gray-blue velvet. Fear for herself, for her weakening defenses, made her shiver.

Tom snaked his arm around her waist and drew her close. "Are you okay?"

"I'm fine," she said, tucking a stray curl behind her ear. If she were smart, she'd have him take her home where she'd lock herself in and settle down with a good book, safe from Tom and her own simmering emotions.

Maybe his attentiveness had mellowed her, but she couldn't allow anything to happen. She'd relax, have fun, but that was all.

"Let's stay awhile and enjoy the music," she said, smiling up at him.

"Great," he said. He tightened his arm around her as they threaded their way through the noisy crowd. She leaned against him, caught up in the festive atmosphere that shimmered around them. Being with Tom made everything sharper, brighter, more alive. What harm was there in giving in to her feelings just this once?

"This looks like the place to be," Tom said. "A real party area."

The tables set in front of the stage were filled with laughing, talking twenty- and thirty-somethings.

"Looks like all the tables are taken," Mary Beth said. Disappointment mixed with relief. Maybe Fate was telling her to take the safe course and go home.

"Hey, Tom, over here." A tall sandy-haired man waved his arms at them.

"Jerry Gordon," Tom said. "I went to law school with him." He looked at her. "Do you mind sitting with them if they have room?"

Memories of the last time she had been with a group of Tom's friends chilled her and she stiffened.

"Well?" he said, still looking at her.

"Sure," she said, shaking off her fears. She'd promised herself she'd have fun. She wouldn't let his friends intimidate her.

"Great to see you again," Jerry Gordon said when they reached his table. He shook Tom's hand. "We have two places here. Join us."

They sat down and introductions were made. Some of the women threw assessing glances at Mary Beth before flirting openly with Tom, apparently dismissing her as competition. She gritted her teeth and moved closer to him.

Three hours later the music ended and the group at the table broke up.

Tom slipped his arm over Mary Beth's shoulders as they strolled down the nearly deserted street to his car. She sighed, too filled with good feelings to protest his intimacy. His friends had made her feel welcome. And Tom had been so attentive.

She glanced at his strong profile and lost her footing on the uneven pavement. Tom steadied her, pulling her closer.

"Are you all right?" he asked.

"I'm perfectly fine."

He chuckled.

Laughing, she freed herself and spread her arms, walking sideways to face him. "I had such fun tonight. Your friends are so funny. I haven't laughed like that in years."

She stopped suddenly. Tom almost collided with her. "Did you have a good time too?"

"Mary Beth," he said, grasping her arms and smiling down at her. "I had a great time just being with you and watching you."

He gathered her against him. The gentle warmth of the early summer night and his closeness dissipated the last of her resolve. She cushioned her head against his firm chest. His heart beat strong and steady against her cheek.

"You should let yourself have fun more often," he said, kissing the top of her head. "You're too serious. You were always too serious. When we were kids it was a challenge to make you laugh, but it was worth it." His low, smooth voice slid over her like warm chocolate.

"You're so cute," she said, surprised at her boldness.

He threw back his head and laughed. "And I think you are very tired and don't know what you're saying."

"I know exactly what I'm saying," she said.

His hands bracketed her waist and he pushed her gently away. "Don't tempt me," he whispered huskily, his gaze soft. "Let's get you home. We both have to work tomorrow."

Ignoring her soft moan of protest, he put his arm around her and guided her along the quiet street.

The minute Tom parked his car in front of her apartment house, Mary Beth unbuckled her seat belt and reached for the door handle. She had been way too forward, letting him hold her. She needed to get away before she made a complete fool of herself.

"Thanks for everything," she said in the most polite voice she could manage. "You don't need to get out of the car."

He arched an eyebrow at her. "I'll walk you to your door." His firm voice allowed no argument.

He cupped her elbow, helping her along the brick pathway and up the steep stairs to the second floor.

"You got me safely home," she said, leaning against her apartment door.

"I hope I didn't keep you out too late," Tom said. He stroked his finger along her cheek. The dim light from the hall lamp cast an intimate glow over his sculpted features.

She studied him, the high cheekbones and straight nose, the deep blue eyes. No man had a right to be that wickedly handsome . . . to make her want to kiss him so badly.

Warning bells sounded in her head. She needed to escape. Fast.

She ran her tongue over her dry lips. Tom's gaze fastened on her mouth.

The alarms rang louder, but she ignored them.

Reaching out a trembling hand, she ran a finger over his full, warm lips. His eyes darkened with a longing that made her want to draw closer. Scared of her own weakness, she backed away instead.

He pulled her to him. She floated on air, wrapped in a bubble of pleasure. His slow, thorough kiss made her fears fly away.

"You're so beautiful," he murmured against her lips.

She wrapped her arms around his neck. "I had such a good time tonight," she whispered. "Why don't you come in for coffee?"

He leaned his forehead against hers. "I want to, but it's late."

Humiliation heated her face. She'd let her guard down and enjoyed a magical evening, one she didn't want to end. Apparently Tom didn't feel the same way. He couldn't wait to get away from her.

She reached down to grab the purse she had dropped and fumbled in it for her keys. She let out a cry of frustration when she failed to find them.

"Mary Beth." He grabbed her shoulders. She twisted her head away from him.

"No," he said. "Look at me, Cat Eyes." He took her chin between his fingers and tilted her face toward his.

She stared up at him. Faint lines etched around his mouth. "I must be crazy," he said, shaking his head, "but it's best if I go now."

He took her purse and reached in to extricate the keys. He handed her the bag and unlocked the door. It swung open at his touch.

She turned quickly, eager to escape into the sanctuary of her apartment.

He pulled her gently around to face him and traced his thumb along her bottom lip. "I had a great time tonight, Cat Eyes."

Chapter Six

Thump! The heavy weight landing on Mary Beth's chest woke her with the force of an electric current. Heart palpitating wildly, she gasped and opened her eyes to bright sunlight and Missy's furry face inches from hers.

The cat wailed a loud "feed me" cry. Pushing her pet gently aside, Mary Beth turned to look at the bedside clock. She groaned as pain, like tiny meat cleavers, stabbed her head.

"Oh, God," she said, settling back on the pillow. She was due at work an hour ago. And it seemed as if she'd only just fallen asleep.

"Oh, God," she moaned again as last night came rushing back to her. Tom. She'd thrown herself at him. Again. And he'd rejected her. Again. Only this time others didn't watch, cheering.

Anger at herself and embarrassment had given her a restless night. She pressed a hand to her queasy stomach and took deep breaths.

The shrill ringing of the phone made her jump. The knives in her head sliced harder.

The answering machine in the living room clicked on. "Mary Beth, are you there?" Tom's voice, loud, urgent, made her wince.

"Pick up right now or I'm coming over."

Tom here? No way, her addled brain cried. Gingerly, with a hand that shook, she reached for the phone next to the bed.

"Yes?" she rasped.

"Are you all right? Gail's been calling you. She's worried sick. So am I."

Mary Beth clutched the receiver and lay back on the bed, trying to ignore the warmth that flooded her at the concern and relief in Tom's voice.

"I-I'm fine," she whispered.

"You don't sound fine," he said. "I'm coming over."

"No!" Sharp pain shot through her head. "Really, I'm okay. I have a wicked headache. I ate too much at the festival and I had trouble sleeping."

"Are you sure it was the food that kept you awake?" he said softly.

No, it was total humiliation, she thought.

"Tell—tell Gail I'll call her," she said. "I have to go now." She replaced the receiver on the cradle and threw the bed covers aside. No lying around feeling sorry for herself.

Mary Beth fed Missy and gave Gail a call. A long, cool shower and three extra-strength aspirin reduced her headache to a dull pounding.

She dressed quickly in loose-fitting black pants and a white T-shirt. She tried to concentrate on the routine tasks, but the memory of last night kept repeating on her like a skipping record. Everything had gone so well. Why did she invite him in for coffee, setting up her own rejection? Living with stress for so long had rendered her temporarily insane, making her fling herself at the first hunk to come along.

She brushed her hair out and began braiding it, staring at her pale reflection in the mirror. Who was she fooling? Tom meant more to her than just a gorgeous guy. A lot more.

She shifted uneasily. The true Tom had emerged that night at the formal, shattering her dreams and locking her heart in an icy cage.

A small kernel of doubt took seed in her mind. Mixed with her humiliation was the knowledge that Tom had been considerate of her all evening, making sure she had a good time, attentive to her in front of his friends. Honorable in every way.

Maybe Tom was right. She should let the past go. Start seeing him in a new light.

Fear made her shiver. If she didn't keep her guard up, Tom would break her heart again. Once she ceased being a challenge to him he'd go back to his own kind, like before. Images of Tom disappearing into Taylor's arms came unbidden to her mind, making her stomach churn.

She squeezed her eyes shut. She was financially dependent on Tom for now. Until she controlled her own finances again, she couldn't allow herself to be involved with any man, especially Tom. Unlike her mother, she would make her own way in the world.

She'd be careful around Tom from now on.

"Very cool," Gail said.

"Very 'Titans of Industry,' " Mary Beth said, following Gail's gaze around the large, luxurious boardroom of Sackett Industries.

Chairs, richly upholstered in creams and hunter green, surrounded the huge mahogany table that dominated the room. Old money whispered from the crown molding, brass chandeliers, and paintings by Andrew and Jamie Wyeth that adorned the dark green walls.

Secretaries scurried in and out, setting packets at each place in preparation for the quarterly directors' meeting. Mary Beth and Gail were catering breakfast and lunch for the Sackett directors and visiting foreign plant managers.

"It even smells like money," Mary Beth said, inhaling the subdued scent of cinnamon potpourri that wafted from porcelain bowls set on the elaborately carved side tables.

"Tom came from this?" Gail's voice was filled with awe.

"This is only the boardroom," Mary Beth said. "Imagine what his parents' house is like."

"You've never been to his house?" Gail said, frowning.

"No," Mary Beth said, with a rueful grin. "Tom and I didn't exactly come from the same social group."

The rich surroundings drove a tiny knife through Mary Beth's heart, a reminder of the differences between her world and Tom's. He may have befriended her once, but when the time came he'd chosen his wealthy friends over her. Old sadness twisted slowly through her.

"Guess we'd better man our stations," Gail said, glancing at her watch.

Mary Beth followed Gail to the marble-floored gathering area where white-clothed tables groaned under the weight of heavy silver coffee urns and homemade pastries and sweets. Almond and vanilla coffee flavors competed with the mouth-watering scents of honey, sugar, cinnamon, and fruit. Uniformed food workers from the Sackett cafeteria stood ready to serve the meeting attendees.

"The Sacketts sure know how to throw a party," Gail said. "Here's Tom now."

Mary Beth swung around. Tom strode quickly toward them, the picture of wealth, power, and virility in his exquisitely tailored charcoal suit and snowy white shirt. Her breath caught in her throat.

His gaze sought hers. He threw her a smile that made her heart tumble against her chest. She hadn't seen him since the Greek Festival five days ago. They'd talked on the phone to discuss the menu for today's meeting, but she had kept their conversations polite and businesslike. There could never be anything more between them.

"Morning," he said, still looking at her. "Everything looks and smells terrific, but I wouldn't expect anything less from my two favorite caterers."

"Good morning," Mary Beth said, summoning all her strength to sound calm. She felt sure Tom could hear the wild thumping of her heart.

"Cozy little place you've got here," Gail said, arching an eyebrow.

"We like it," he said, laughing.

"It is pretty fabulous," Mary Beth said, focusing on a luxurious Oriental rug that adorned a portion of the marble floor. Tom's closeness and the familiar subtle scent of his cologne mixed a dangerous brew that threatened her control.

"The others should be arriving soon," he said. "Do you have everything you need? Any questions?"

"We're fine," Mary Beth said, glancing at him. "Your staff's been great."

"Can't wait to taste your Maryland crab cakes at lunch," he said.

"The crab cakes are one of Mary Beth's specialties," Gail said. "Let's hope they're a hit with your guests."

"They will be." Tom's mouth tipped upwards in a smile. "The Bennetts are still raving about the meal you prepared for them."

Jealousy, like a bitter herb, made Mary Beth's stomach cramp. The Bennetts. No doubt Tom and Taylor spent time together. She chewed her lip. So what. She didn't care about his personal life.

"Mary Beth, can I talk to you a minute?" Tom's gaze probed hers. "Alone."

Mary Beth swallowed. Excitement and apprehension balled in her chest. "Gail needs me," she said, clutching at any excuse to avoid being alone with him.

"Don't worry about me," Gail said. "Everything's all set here. Go ahead."

Mary Beth gave Gail a look before Tom cupped her elbow to lead her to a quiet corner of the large room.

"What do you want to discuss that Gail can't hear?" She tried to sound cool but she couldn't mask the huskiness that softened her voice.

He still held onto her elbow, standing so close she could see the light shadings of a beard on his clean-shaven face. God, he looked good. She tamped down the crazy urge to slide her fingers over his smooth lapel and trail a path to his firm jaw.

"We have to talk about the other night, after the festival," he said. "Unless you want me to invite Gail over to listen." He raised an eyebrow.

"No!" Her face burned. "There is nothing to discuss. We ate great food. Lots of great food. And we had a good time. That's all."

"Just be quiet and listen to me for once." His gaze held hers. "I wanted to come in for coffee. But I didn't trust myself alone with you. I accompanied you to the festival because I wanted to be with you, not for any ulterior motive. I didn't want you getting the wrong idea."

Could she believe him? She lifted her chin. "It's okay, Tom." She'd never let him guess the humiliation she had felt that night.

He relaxed his stance. "No hard feelings then?"

She shook her head.

He kept staring at her, making her fidget. She had to get away so she could breathe normally again.

"I have work to do," she said, turning.

"Not so fast." He gently pulled her back.

He stroked his finger along her jaw with the merest whisper of a touch. "Just because I left doesn't mean I don't want to be with you. I do. A lot. And I think you feel the same about me."

She looked quickly away before he saw the answering awareness in her eyes.

Muted voices reached them, becoming louder as the first of the meeting attendees rounded the corner.

"I have to go," she said, relieved to escape before she made a fool of herself again.

"We'll talk later," he said.

"I think not." She turned and walked away.

"What was that all about?" Gail asked when Mary Beth joined her at the head table.

She shrugged. "Nothing."

"You're a terrible liar," Gail said.

"Don't push it, Gail. I still haven't forgiven you for setting me up to go to the festival with Tom."

"You didn't mind as much as you pretend."

"Can it." She narrowed her eyes at Gail.

"We'll continue this later," Gail said. "Brace yourself. The locusts are descending."

The reception area quickly filled with men and women, all dressed in business suits. Briefcases had been left in the conference room, freeing them to enjoy the coffee, juice, and sweets.

Subdued voices, foreign and American, floated to Mary Beth's ears. The delicate fragrances of expensive perfumes mingled with the pungent-sweet scents of the coffee and pastries.

Gail nudged her. "Look at the Viking," she said. "And he's heading this way."

A well-built blond man shouldered his way through the crowd. His sophisticated carriage and the stylish cut of his clothes shouted European tailoring.

"Ladies," he said when he reached them. His gaze shifted between the women, resting on Mary Beth.

"Kurt von Zuben. Plant manager of the Munich branch." He spoke with a thick German accent. His sleek, practiced smile made the hairs on Mary Beth's neck stiffen.

"Mary Beth Kendrick," she said coolly.

"Gail O'Connell," Gail said.

"Two beautiful women who cook like angels. Only in America."

His pale silver gaze ran up and down Mary Beth, making her shiver. "I have a weakness for redheads," he said. "Especially beautiful ones." His charm-filled voice slid over Mary Beth like bad cooking oil.

"I am here in your wonderful city for only three weeks," he said to her. "Perhaps you will show me around. I promise you a good time."

"Von Zuben." Tom appeared at the man's side. His jaw was set in a tight line. "There's someone I want you to meet." He ushered the man away.

The German glanced back at Mary Beth. "We will talk later," he said.

"Everyone wants to talk to me later," she muttered. "I don't intend to be anywhere near here once lunch is over."

"Good morning, Mrs. Hagerty." Tom's deep voice could be heard from the reception area.

Mary Beth's hands froze over the stuffed capons she was about to put into the roasting pan. She turned slowly to face the doorway.

"Are they both in?" she heard him ask.

"Just Ms. Kendrick."

"Good. I have an important meeting with Ms. Kendrick. We'd appreciate it if we weren't disturbed."

"Of course, Mr. Sackett."

Tom strode quickly into the kitchen. Mary Beth scanned his tall, muscular form, clad in tight jeans and an open-necked denim shirt that revealed a triangle of dark hair. Emotion rose up in her throat. She leaned against the counter for support.

"I'm doing better at announcing myself," he said. "I didn't startle you this time."

"No, but you surprised me. What was that about a meeting? If it's business, Gail won't be back for another hour."

"Oh, it's business all right, but it concerns just the two of us." He walked slowly toward her, a gleam in his eyes. The counter edge pressed into her back.

A shaft of midmorning sunlight lit her face. She shivered, despite the warmth.

"Are you cold?" he asked.

"No." She slid away from him to the other end of the long counter. He didn't follow.

"Why are you here?" She took deep breaths and willed her fluttering heart to settle down.

He folded his arms across his chest. The sunlight winked off the stainless steel links of his expensive watch. Nature's little reminder of the differences between her and Tom.

"I'm on my way to the airport," he said. "Some problems at our Pittsburgh plant. I'm the only one available to go up there to straighten things out. I'll be back in time for my parents' party in two weeks. I had to see you before I left."

Some of the air escaped Mary Beth's lungs at the thought of two weeks without Tom and his disturbing, though exciting, presence.

His gaze scanned her face. "The meeting took longer than I expected yesterday and I didn't get a chance to talk to you," he said and smiled. "By the way, your food was a big hit. We reviewed your business plan and potential earnings, and after tasting your food, I look like a hero for bringing your company into the Sackett fold."

Mary Beth relaxed. She could handle talking business with him. "That's great. Gail and I know our food is terrific, but we need validation from our customers. And we like people to enjoy our cooking."

"Some of the men enjoyed more than your food," he said. His jaw tightened.

"What?"

"Stay away from von Zuben. He's bad news."

Anger stiffened her spine. "You may run my business, but you don't run my life."

Frustration and determination filled Tom's chiseled features. "I am not telling you what to do, or who to see. It's just that von Zuben is trouble. I don't want you mixed up with him. He's not your type."

"How do you know?" she said, placing her hand on her hip.

He moved closer. Her breath faltered.

"You're not the casual affair type. Von Zuben is looking for a little action while he's here. He has a fiancée back in Munich."

"Maybe I don't care if he has a fiancée. Maybe I enjoy casual affairs." Indignation made her reckless. She'd never consider dating the smooth-talking German, but she wouldn't let Tom know that.

"Then you plan to go out with him?" His voice was strained.

"That's none of your business," she said, thrusting her chin out.

He flinched. "It is none of my business." He closed the gap between them until he stood directly in front of her. Her heart did crazy little flips.

His features softened. "No, you won't go out with him." He twisted his hand around her braid and pulled her gently toward him. "You're not his type, Cat Eyes."

"Whose type am I?" she whispered.

"My type," he rasped.

She knew she should back away, but the fire in his deep blue eyes held her.

"While I'm gone," he said, placing his hands on her shoulders, "I want you to remember something if von Zuben or any other man comes around."

"Remember what?" she asked, breathlessly.

"This."

His mouth captured hers in a kiss that shattered her world. Self-preserving fear fought with the excitement that sang through her bones. She clenched her hands against his chest, battling the magnetism that drew her under his spell.

Tom's deliberate possession of her mouth pushed aside her defenses. Feelings she didn't want to acknowledge gnawed around the edges of her soul, demanding release.

What little resistance she had crumbled in a heap at her feet. She melted against him, savoring his warmth and his faint taste of peppermint and coffee.

He trailed kisses down her neck to the base of her throat. "So sweet," he murmured against her skin.

The past, the present, the world dissolved, leaving her in a magical place where only she and Tom existed. All that mattered, all she knew, was Tom's closeness and warmth. She slid her arms around his neck, twining her fingers in the thickness of his crisp hair.

The jangling of the front doorbell, followed by the secretary's melodic greeting, penetrated Mary Beth's brain like soft whispers waking her from a wonderful dream. She refused to wake up.

The voices continued, poking into her consciousness until the dream and the magic popped like a champagne cork.

With a soft cry, she pushed away. Tom grasped her upper arms. His breathing was harsh and his blue eyes looked tormented.

Her heart beat with such ferocity that she felt sure Tom could see it pumping against her chest. She tucked her bottom lip between her teeth, unable to talk, barely able to breathe.

They stared at each other for long seconds. Tom dropped his arms to his sides. A short laugh escaped him.

"The joke's on me, Cat Eyes," he said in a husky voice.

"Joke?" she said, her voice quivering.

"I intended to kiss you so thoroughly that you

wouldn't even look at another man while I'm gone." He smoothed a shaky hand over his hair.

"Instead," he said, skimming his long, slender finger down her cheekbone to her mouth, "I'm the one who will be lying awake in a lonely hotel room, missing you. The next two weeks will be torture."

He bent to brush a soft kiss across her lips, then turned abruptly and strode away.

Mary Beth sagged back against the counter. "Darn you," she whispered to his retreating back.

Chapter Seven

"Where should I put this, Ms. Kendrick?"

"Set it on the table over there, Janice. Thanks."

Mary Beth directed the teenage server to one of several wooden tables set up on the spacious lawn of the Sackett estate.

Sighing deeply, she scanned the rolling property, exquisitely landscaped with ornamental and exotic trees and shrubs. Colorful wildflowers grew in designed abandon.

After all these years she was finally at Tom's parents' house. She'd always dreamed of being invited. Of course, her fantasies didn't include being there as the hired help.

She smiled. Not exactly hired help. She and Gail had scored the most sought-after catering contract of the season—the Sackett family's annual cookout.

Excitement skittered up her spine as she surveyed the groups of chattering, well-dressed guests, the cream of Wilmington and Philadelphia society. They sat at round tables under bright blue umbrellas and wandered in and out of the large yellow-and-white-striped tent where a three-piece string ensemble played chamber music.

Humming softly, Mary Beth turned to the table behind her. Small crystal bowls were stacked next to a larger one brimming with fresh fruit. She separated the bowls and began arranging them around the fruit.

After today, Kendrick and Company would be on its way to becoming the caterer of choice among Wilmington's glitterati. Things couldn't be better . . . working in a beautiful place with charming people, doing the job she loved, and doing it well. She skimmed her finger over the fine etchings on one of the bowls. Her happiness could fill all the dishes on the table.

The truth nudged her. Business success wasn't the only reason for the joy that had been with her from the minute she woke up. Tom. He was due back from Pittsburgh. She'd missed him more than she liked to admit. He made her laugh and smile and feel happier than she had in a long time.

Soon he'd come striding confidently through the crowd. To her. Her stomach clenched in delicious anticipation.

Stepping back, she surveyed her handiwork. She rubbed her fingers over her lips, the table setting forgotten, as memories of Tom's shattering kiss two weeks ago burned into her. Since then her waking hours had been filled with him and her dreams had been free of the outside world and its problems.

"Ms. Kendrick, I need your help."

Startled out of her sweet reverie, Mary Beth turned in the direction of the frantic teenager's voice. Kate. She smiled. The girl was a doll, but so clumsy.

"Be right there, Kate," she called out.

She moved a bowl a quarter inch and, satisfied, started toward the hapless teen.

She spotted Taylor Bennett and Tom's very pregnant sister Maureen walking in her direction. Their heads, one blond, one raven, were bent together in conversation.

Wistfulness twisted inside Mary Beth. She'd never belong to the rarefied world of the Sacketts and Bennetts. Pride steeled her. She didn't need or want their world.

Tom's sister threw her a friendly smile. Maureen's eyes, so like Tom's, sparkled with interest as her gaze swept over Mary Beth. Taylor smoothed back her sleek platinum hair with fuchsia-tipped fingers and slid Mary Beth a glance, a smug smile on her lips.

"I can't wait till next weekend," Taylor said to Maureen. "Tommy and I will be together at the shore for three whole days." Her words, loud and clear over the buzz of the crowd, sawed through Mary Beth like a rusty blade.

Tripping on the uneven ground, Mary Beth swayed

against a wooden serving cart. The air seemed to be sucked out of her lungs as if she were caught in a tornado. The vivid colors of the wildflowers and the bright clothes worn by the guests blurred, making her dizzy.

"Ms. Kendrick. Please. I need you."

While a part of her helped Kate clean up the spill, directed some of the serving crew, and smiled at guests, Mary Beth's soul screamed in stunned disbelief.

Tom and Taylor spending a weekend together. He had toyed with her. Again. Anger and humiliation boiled inside her.

She sank into a nearby chair and swiped at the sweat beading on her forehead. The sun still rode high in the sky, but storm clouds covered her heart.

She'd dreamed of Tom, hungered to touch him, to watch the play of sunlight on his black hair, to see him smile, hear him laugh, kiss him. But he wasn't coming home to her. Taylor and her high society life still claimed him.

Gripping the wide arm of the chair, Mary Beth fought the nausea that was snaking its way from her stomach to her throat.

At least this time she was spared public humiliation. No one knew of her dashed hopes. She should be grateful to Taylor for showing her where she stood with Tom. Betrayal the second time around would be too much to bear.

"Here. Drink this." Gail appeared in front of her,

thrusting a large frosted glass of water at her. A lemon wedge floated along the top.

"Thanks." She took the glass with a shaky hand and gulped the cool, citrus-flavored liquid.

"Your face is as white as that chair," Gail said. "What happened?"

"Nothing I want to talk about."

"Well get a grip," Gail said. "Von Zuben's looking for you. And Tom's here." She nodded toward the tent.

Tom. A pang of joy, quickly suppressed, jolted Mary Beth. Taking a long sip of water, she forced herself to stand slowly. Handing her half-empty glass to a passing waiter, she composed her face into what she hoped was a calm mask.

"I can barely get through this party now, let alone deal with Kurt's leering. It's bad enough that he hung around our place the last two weeks trying to get a date with me." She twisted her hand around her braid. "And I couldn't care less about Tom. Besides, we're working."

"Touchy, touchy," Gail said, arching an eyebrow. "We can take it easy for awhile. Things are humming along nicely. The guests are happily marinated with alcohol and the barbecue chefs are grilling up filet mignons to die for."

"I prefer to keep busy," Mary Beth said. Despite her resolve to push Tom from her mind, her gaze wandered to the tent.

Tom, flanked by his parents, stood with a small

group of talking, laughing people. Mary Beth's gaze drank in the sight him, absorbing every detail like a wilted flower thirsty for sustenance.

The khaki shorts he wore showed off his long muscular legs. His white T-shirt stretched across his broad chest. His slightly disheveled hair and the lines of fatigue fingering his mouth made him look vulnerable. Achingly vulnerable.

She pressed a hand to her stomach, fighting the craving that made her want to throw herself in his arms, to smooth the tired planes of his face.

Taylor's revelations slammed into her mind. Anger hit her with the swiftness of a summer storm. She dug her nails into her palms.

Tom drew apart from the group surrounding him and scanned the crowd. Probably looking for Taylor. Jealousy, like a poker, jabbed Mary Beth in the ribs.

The sweet scent of barbecue sauce and the pungent odor of roasting meat, so enjoyable moments ago, sickened her. So did the image of Tom and Taylor spending a weekend together.

Her anger and hurt couldn't stop her gaze from seeking his across the rolling lawn. He threw her a smile that caressed. Her breath caught; her mind filled with confusion. Just being near Tom rattled her completely.

He headed in her direction, moving with the easy grace she knew so well. Her heart beat wildly in her chest.

"Mary Beth, you have been avoiding me."

She started. Kurt von Zuben stood at her elbow.

"Kurt, I told you earlier that I was busy."

"How busy will you be now that Sackett has returned?" Amusement lit his silver eyes.

"That doesn't concern you," she said.

Tom approached, a scowl on his face.

"Von Zuben," he said. "Still bothering the ladies? Can't you see they're working?"

Apparently Tom considered her just an employee. Resentment and hurt collided in Mary Beth, making her stiffen.

"They don't seem to mind, Sackett," Kurt said.

The men glared at each other.

"Glad you could make it, Tom," Gail said, positioning herself between the two men.

"Gail." Tom nodded.

He looked past her to Mary Beth. "How have you been, Mary Beth?"

The huskiness of his voice and the heat in his eyes sent delicious shivers up her spine.

She squared her shoulders, determined to resist his pull.

"I'm fine, Tom. How was your trip?" She struggled to sound impersonal.

"The trip was rough," he said, frowning. His questioning gaze threatened her fragile control.

She wanted to brush away the raven lock of hair that fell over his forehead, tell him how much she missed him.

Holding her body rigid, she let anger seep in. He would be with Taylor next weekend.

Mary Beth turned away quickly. She grabbed salad utensils from the table and began tossing the mixed greens that filled a large ceramic bowl. Her hands shook. Vegetables flew off the forks and onto the table. Counting to ten, she forced herself to calm down.

"Have you sampled the food?" she heard Gail ask.

"I haven't eaten yet," Tom said. "But my parents and their guests are raving about the food. You two are a hit, as usual."

Mary Beth could feel Tom's stare boring into her back, but she refused to look at him.

"These angels of the kitchen are magnificent cooks," Kurt said in his clipped German accent.

"Kurt's been around our shop so much in the past two weeks that he's become our official taster," Gail said.

"The food wasn't the only appeal," von Zuben answered.

Mary Beth could feel Kurt's stare too, but she continued to work, carefully measuring out salad into smaller dishes.

"We need to talk, von Zuben. I told you to keep your distance."

The menacing tone of Tom's voice made Mary Beth's pulse quicken. She swung around to look at him. His mouth was set in a tight line. Tension throbbed between the two men.

Mary Beth frowned. Tom couldn't possibly be jeal-

ous. He didn't care about her. He was just worried
about spoiling his mother's party. Sadness pulled at
her insides.

"Tommy, darling, there you are."

Taylor slinked slowly across the lawn toward them.
The skimpy white dress she wore showed off the perfection of her long, tanned body.

Bile rose in Mary Beth's throat. She couldn't stand
to see Taylor with Tom, to see her fuchsia-tipped fingers stroke his bare arm.

"I have work to do," she said, walking quickly
away.

"Mary Beth. Wait." Tom caught up with her, grabbing her arm and pulling her around to face him.

"What's wrong?" he said. "We have to talk." The
longing in his eyes weakened her resolve.

"I'm busy," she said, pulling free before she could
give in to her own needs and hold him close. "This is
an important job."

Chin high, she strode away. Her heart seemed to
crack in two. Just when the wounds of the past had
started to dissolve, when she had begun to trust Tom
again. . . .

She balled her fists, fighting the bitterness and pain.
She couldn't let him know how much the thought of
him and Taylor together hurt.

Tom watched her graceful, hip-swaying exit. His
heart thudded in his chest.

He had missed Mary Beth so much in the past two
weeks that he thought he'd go crazy if he didn't see

her, touch her, kiss her. Her flashing green eyes, wide smile, and sultry voice had kept him awake many nights.

Instead of the joyous, heated reunion he'd anticipated, he'd been greeted with enough ice to freeze his parents' swimming pool. What was wrong now? If her coldness had anything to do with von Zuben . . . no, he couldn't think about that.

He wanted to run after her, make her talk to him, look at him with warmth instead of ice chips in her eyes. But he knew better than to push her. For whatever reason, she needed her space. He'd give it to her, for now.

"I've got to get a life," Mary Beth muttered. She stared out her apartment window to the almost-deserted street. It seemed everyone was someplace else this July Fourth. Even her mother was with friends.

Her mother. Mary Beth smoothed her hair with one hand and shook her head. Since her mom had started working at the florist shop, she'd bloomed like the flowers she tended. Her mother had actually planned a visit to Aunt Linda in Arizona next month. The woman had a more active social life than she did.

And Tom was at the shore with Taylor. All day the thought had been pounding at her like the ocean surf. Images of the couple laughing, walking on the beach, sharing intimate moments, washed over her in waves of hurt and anger.

"Darn it." She stamped her foot. Her cat, stretched out on the wide, sunny windowsill, opened one green eye to stare at her.

"I'm a jerk, Missy. Why am I alone on a holiday, obsessing over Tom and Taylor?"

She had to get a grip. She and Tom had shared a few kisses. So what? As long as her company thrived, it didn't matter who he spent time with.

Liar, liar, a tiny voice prodded. She paced the small living room, trying to ease the frustration that ate at her.

Tom hadn't called her once in the five days since the cookout. Not once.

"It's just your ego that's bruised," she said to the quiet room. "Get over it."

Squaring her shoulders, she headed for the bedroom. She refused to sit around pining like a lovesick teen. She'd go to Gail's party after all.

The doorbell buzzed. She jumped. Probably Gail, coming over in person to persuade her to get out and have some fun.

She pressed the button allowing her to talk to whoever was downstairs.

"Alright, Gail. You win. I'll be there."

A deep chuckle came over the line. She jerked away as if burned.

"I'm sure Gail would be glad to hear that," a male voice shot back.

Tom. Joy and apprehension made her stomach tense.

"What do you want?" she said.

"I need to see you. You going to let me in?"

"Go. . . ." She stopped. She wasn't afraid of him or her own feelings. They had business between them. Nothing more.

"Come up." She buzzed him in and opened her apartment door to wait.

Heavy footsteps creaked up the stairs, then he was in the room, shutting the door quietly behind him.

They stared at each other. Her breath faltered. She had missed him these last weeks . . . missed his smile, the way his deep blue eyes crinkled at the corners when he laughed. She'd hungered for his nearness, for the way he made even the most routine tasks more vivid. And mostly for the way he made her feel—more alive than she'd ever been in her life.

She folded her arms across her chest as protection from the warmth that swept over her.

"What do you want?" she said again.

Tom gave her a dazzling smile that made her stomach twist in knots. "We've been through that already." He held up a large plastic bag. "Can I put this somewhere? It's getting heavy."

"What is it?"

"Dinner. Chinese. I got hungry on the way over. I thought you might be too."

"Put it on the table," she said, nodding toward the dining area.

Her gaze followed his long-legged strides across the room. His jeans and gray T-shirt hugged the muscular contours of his body. The tall, skinny kid she once knew sure filled a pair of denims now. The thought made her face burn.

"Let's eat," he said. "Where are your dishes?"

"Not so fast." She narrowed her eyes. He couldn't just breeze in here, as if nothing had happened between them, as if he hadn't planned a romantic weekend with another woman.

"Why are you here, Tom? I thought you were away."

"No." He shook his head. "The Bennetts invited me to their place in Stone Harbor. They wanted me to meet some people who are interested in doing business with our company."

His deep blue gaze studied her. "But I had something more important to do," he finished.

Her pulse quickened. "Then you're not going to the shore with Taylor?"

Mary Beth cringed inwardly and wanted to bite the words back. Relief had weakened her, sabotaging her defenses.

He frowned. "What made you think that?"

"Something I heard," she said, shrugging. The rapid beating of her heart threatened the outward calmness she was trying to project.

An amused gleam lit Tom's eyes as he slowly walked toward her.

"Jealous?" he said, tugging gently on her braid and pulling her closer.

"No!" She jerked free.

He laughed softly.

"I'll get the dishes," she said, hurrying into the kitchen.

"Need any help?" he asked.

"No. Stay there."

"You're a coward, Mary Beth Kendrick. You always run from the truth."

"I'm not running." She clamped her mouth shut. It didn't matter what he thought. She wasn't a teenager anymore. She could handle Tom. And Taylor.

Anger churned inside her. The cunning blond had humiliated her for the last time.

She pulled open a cabinet door and grabbed two plates, then threw silverware onto them. The stainless steel clinked against the ceramic.

"You tearing the place apart?" Tom called out from the other room.

"I'm fine. Just clumsy."

Leaning against the counter, Mary Beth took deep breaths. Tom showing up today meant nothing. He was probably here on business. That was fine with her.

Liar, liar, the little voice mocked. "Oh, shut up," she muttered.

"Food's good," Tom said a few minutes later. He pushed a forkful of plum duck into his mouth.

Mary Beth skimmed her finger over the rim of her water goblet and tried to ignore the happiness stirring in her. Her need to be near Tom, to touch him and talk to him, grew stronger each time she saw him. Excitement made her stomach tighten.

She pushed a piece of steamed shrimp around the plate with her fork. Even the sweet-spicy odors of the delicious-looking food couldn't entice her to eat. Her appetite had dissolved in the heady joy of seeing Tom, of being with him.

"I've missed you," he said softly.

She looked up to find him staring at her. The attraction that always bubbled around them rose to the surface. Immersed in the blue of his eyes, she couldn't look away. Her fork dropped from her hand and hit the plate with a loud ring, breaking the spell.

"I wanted to call you," he said, "but I knew you needed your space. Then Maureen had her baby and I had to help with her other kids. I couldn't get away till now."

"You were baby-sitting?" The Tom she used to know wouldn't have had the patience to care for small children.

The corners of his mouth turned up in a wry smile. "Believe it or not, my sister trusts me with her kids."

"That's not what I meant," she said.

"Of course it is," he said, laughing. "But that's okay." His gaze caressed her. "There's a lot about me you don't know."

"Are they okay?" she blurted out. "Maureen and the baby, I mean." She shifted, trying to tamp down the warmth spreading through her at the tenderness of his gaze.

His wide smile made him look younger and more

vulnerable, like the Tom she had loved so long ago. Her heart did a tiny flip.

"They're both great. Maureen and Robert have a beautiful little girl who looks just like her mother."

"I'm glad," she said. "They must be very happy."

"They are." He leaned closer. "Why haven't you ever married, Cat Eyes?"

She bristled. "No time. Why haven't you married?"

"I was engaged once." Pain shadowed his face.

"Engaged?" She swallowed around the lump in her throat.

He brushed his hand over his hair and shifted in his chair. "Clarice was one of my partners in the storefront law office we operated in the Bronx."

"Storefront office?"

"We were very idealistic," he said. "But we helped a lot of people. I'm proud of that."

She widened her eyes. "You? A charity office? Why?"

He shot her a rueful smile. "I know that's hard to believe, but I had my reasons. Someday I'll tell you about them."

Mary Beth pushed her plate away and pressed her palms on the table. Revelations about this new, improved Tom made her head reel. Baby-sitting? Doing public charity? She'd sort out her jumbled feelings later. She couldn't concentrate with him sitting opposite her.

"What happened to your engagement?" She wasn't sure she'd like the answer, but she had to know.

"She dumped me for Jack, our other partner."

"Oh." He must still love this Clarice. Mary Beth's hopes sank like the stones she used to throw in the Delaware River when she was a kid.

"That must have hurt," she said in a strained voice.

He picked up his glass of iced tea and stared at the golden brown liquid. "Their betrayal hurt. They were my best friends and they carried on an affair right under my nose."

"I'm sorry, Tom." He knew how betrayal felt. Had that helped change him from the spoiled boy she remembered to the kind, generous man he now seemed to be?

She blinked her eyes, trying to squash her traitorous thoughts. Regardless of how Tom had changed, she couldn't let him into her heart again. The pain of his rejection would be more than she could take.

He slid his glance back to her. "Don't be too sorry. I already knew that I had to come home, that I couldn't marry Clarice, but I didn't want to hurt her. God knows, I'd done enough hurting in my life."

Mary Beth looked quickly away. She had lived with the old, painful memories, believing the worst of him, for so long. This new image of Tom was hard to absorb. And dangerous.

"Enough about me," he said, drawing her attention back to him. "Why the deep freeze at the cookout? I thought we had an understanding before I left for Pittsburgh."

Tension tightened her stomach. "The only under-standing we have is that you're my boss."

"Boss?" His jaw clenched. "I'm not your boss."

She fought the urge to smooth away the tension from his mouth, to tell him he meant so much more. She choked back the perilous words.

"There's just business between us." She sounded unconvincing even to herself.

The intensity of his gaze made her flinch. "There's way more than business between us, Mary Beth. And you know it."

Pushing his plate away, he leaned forward. "You can't keep denying the truth."

"I'm not denying anything," she said.

"Then tell me why the cold shoulder at my parents."

"I had work to do. I was preoccupied. Nothing else."

"Stubborn to the end," he said, shaking his head.

"Think what you will," she said.

"It's not because of von Zuben, is it?"

"Don't be ridiculous. Not that it's any of your con-cern."

His features relaxed. "It's my concern, all right, but we won't go there now." He settled into his chair, his gaze never leaving hers.

She angled her chin. "How did you know I'd be home today?"

"Gail told me. Said you didn't even want to go to her party."

"I've got to have a talk with that woman."

Tom laughed. His eyes crinkled at the corners. She'd always loved his easy laugh. In school, a smile from him, a teasing word, brightened her day. She had thought she knew a sensitive side of him he didn't show to many others, but his betrayal had proved her wrong. Maybe she'd been right all along. Or was she in danger of making the same mistake again?

She grabbed her glass and tossed back the last of the water, wanting to wash away the feelings that weakened her and made her prey to heartbreak.

She stood up. She needed to get away. Tom knew her too well, and he knew how to chip away at her defenses.

"Thanks for the food," she said. "I'm going to Gail's party after all. I have to get ready."

"She invited me too," he said. "I told her I had other plans, but we can go together."

"Together?" Going to a party with Tom would be too much like a . . . date. She wasn't ready for that.

"If you don't want to go to the party, we can go to the fireworks at Rockford Park," he said. "Since Gail's not expecting us, it won't be a problem."

Mary Beth swallowed. Fireworks seemed less like a date. She ignored her racing pulse that told her she and Tom ignited enough sparks to make their own fireworks.

"Okay," she said, letting her breath out. "The park it is. But we go as friends, right?"

"Of course." The amused tilt of his mouth set off warning bells in her head.

"I have to change into a pair of slacks," she said.

"Why? You look terrific in those shorts. Better than terrific."

His appreciative gaze lingered on her. The light in his eyes drew out her need and longing, threatening her self-control and her pride.

He rounded the table to stand directly in front of her. Wrapping his hand around her braid, he pulled her closer until his face was inches from hers.

"Maybe we should stay here and make our own fireworks," he said in a thick voice.

Her breath seemed to stop. It would be so easy to give in, to forget all the old hurts.

The nagging voice of fear slammed into her. If she opened to him again, she'd never be free. Her heart would belong to Tom forever.

She pulled away. "The only fireworks you'll see tonight are at Rockford."

His soft laugh followed her into the bedroom.

Chapter Eight

Business or pleasure? The thought seared through Mary Beth's mind as she and Tom entered the sprawling park. She glanced up at him. His firm jaw spoke of a strength and masculinity that made her heart flip-flop. Her feelings about him were becoming less business and more pleasure every day. Apprehension and heat melded in her stomach.

When Tom slid his hand into hers, a current of excitement shot through her, making her stumble. He tightened his grip and their eyes met.

The intensity in his sapphire eyes acknowledged the charged atmosphere sizzling between them. Embarrassment burned through her and she looked quickly away. His soft laugh, rich and thick, enveloped her in a sultry mix of longing and fear.

Several people in the crowd smiled at them as if

they were a couple. Mary Beth stiffened and pulled her hand from his. What was she thinking? She and Tom weren't a couple, and never would be, if she had any sense. But she was losing all sense where he was concerned. If she weren't careful, she'd lose her heart again too.

"Let's set up here," he said, stopping at a spot thickly carpeted with grass and large enough for the plaid blanket they'd brought from Mary Beth's apartment.

Around them, others were setting up lawn chairs, staking out where they would watch the fireworks that would begin at dark.

Mary Beth settled onto the blanket and drew her knees up close to her body, wrapping her arms around them. Tom sat next to her, only inches away. She felt too vulnerable, too exposed, to look at him. She had to control her longing for him, a longing that threatened to overwhelm and weaken her. Despite his new depth and maturity, she couldn't allow herself to trust him.

"You're awfully quiet," he said. She looked at him. The air around them grew heavy. Slowly, deliberately, he scanned her face, stopping at her mouth.

Her resolve to distance herself from him flew away on the gentle breeze that touched her bare shoulders and ruffled his hair. She slid her hand across the blanket toward him, wanting to caress his sculpted face, to brush aside the stray curl that fell over his forehead.

He leaned closer. Delicious anticipation made her breath catch.

"Ice cream! Get your ice cream here!" Mary Beth jumped up at the vendor's loud cry.

She gulped air and smoothed a shaking hand over her hair. Groups of men, women, and children milled around. She and Tom were in a public place. What had possessed her?

"I need something cold," she said. She clamped her mouth shut. Her face burned.

Tom laughed and stood up slowly. "I know I could use some cooling off."

She swallowed and turned away to head quickly down the small slope toward the ice cream vendor, a large cooler supported by a thick strap slung over his shoulder.

"Why don't we walk around while we eat these," she said after they'd purchased cups of Italian ice.

Taking a small scoop of the lemon-flavored treat, she glanced back at the blanket. Self-protection made her hurry away from the plaid square of temptation and into the crowd.

They strolled on the springy grass, sidestepping blankets and lawn chairs. Mary Beth concentrated on her dessert, but the frozen concoction couldn't cool the emotion that simmered in the air between them.

She forced her thoughts from Tom and focused on the smiling faces of the crowd. Little children clung to brightly colored balloons. Most of the children and some adults wore lightsticks around their necks. Once darkness fell, the sticks would glow neon bright, giving the park an otherworldly feel.

"This is fun," Tom said. "I'm glad we decided to come."

"Are you?" she said.

"Definitely." The bold challenge in his eyes shook her and she slid her glance away. She felt his gaze on her but resisted the impulse to look at him.

"I'd forgotten how good water ice is," he said. "I haven't had one since I was a kid when my Uncle Kevin used to sneak me into Little Italy."

"Sneak you?" Mary Beth glanced at him and lost her footing, tripping on some small stones.

Tom held onto her elbow, steadying her. Someone jostled him from behind and he bumped against her, sending her cup of water ice flying out of her hand onto the ground.

"Oh," she said, staring down at the remnants of her treat and then up at Tom.

"I'm sorry, Mary Beth."

"It wasn't your fault," she said, shrugging. "But it was so good."

He laughed. "Have some of mine." He took a spoonful of the iced treat and held it to her lips.

He stood so close, she could feel his warm breath on her cheeks. Shivers of pleasure danced up her spine.

She opened her mouth and took the food he offered. Closing her lips around the spoon, she savored the tart sweetness.

Tom's gaze held hers. She couldn't look away. She released the spoon.

He scooped up more of the lemon ice and slid it into his own mouth. Mary Beth watched his lips wrap around the spoon. Her insides liquefied. She wanted to taste him, to savor his warmth and masculinity.

"Good, isn't it?" he said softly.

She swallowed, mesmerized by the fire in the depths of his eyes.

A group of children ran past. One of them knocked against her, jarring her back to reality and giving her a heavy dose of embarrassment.

She blew her breath out and lowered her gaze. "I guess we'd better keep walking," she said.

"I guess so," he said, a note of regret in his voice. "Do you want more?" He held out the cup.

She shook her head. "No. Thank you."

"Take it," he said, thrusting the paper cup at her. "I spilled yours. You can have mine." He stooped to pick up the one she'd dropped. "There must be a trash barrel around here somewhere," he said.

Nervousness made her finish Tom's ice quickly as they walked. She had to get some semblance of control over her crazy emotions. Her feelings for Tom were as mixed as the odors wafting through the dusky park—sweet scents of freshly mown grass, flowers, and cotton candy, heavier smells of grilled hot dogs and hamburgers. Lightness and dark. Warmth and passion.

She shook her head to clear it. She really had to get a grip.

"My parents never took me here when I was little," Tom said. "They always brought someone in to do fireworks on our property. I would have enjoyed this."

Mary Beth looked up at him. "Why did your uncle sneak you into Little Italy?" she asked, suddenly remembering the conversation they'd left dangling.

He gave her a wry smile. "My parents felt certain parts of the city weren't suitable for me. But Uncle Kevin felt differently." His face softened. "He was really cool."

She glanced down at the ground, trying to digest what he'd told her. Her heart tugged for the little boy who had to sneak to enjoy one of the city's most popular treats. The boy who wasn't allowed to mingle with the crowd at Rockford Park on July Fourth. Growing up rich wasn't without its problems, she thought.

"There's a trash barrel," he said.

She handed him her empty cup and spoon and watched his long-legged gait across the grass toward the trash receptacle. His lithe agility made the men around him look like overblown dumplings.

Her heart bumped against her chest. God, he was beautiful. At one time she thought he might be hers.

Sadness clutched her and she sighed. They weren't eighteen anymore. She had to remember the lesson of his betrayal and not open herself to hurt again. Ever.

"Tommy, darling." The familiar, pretentious voice made Mary Beth grit her teeth.

Taylor Bennett, looking like a fifties movie star in skintight black capris, black slides, and a small khaki top, slithered toward Tom. *Give me a break,* Mary Beth thought.

Taylor slipped her arm through his and looked up at him, fluttering her thick lashes. White-hot anger scorched Mary Beth. She walked slowly toward them. She refused to let the bleached blond intimidate her.

Tom smiled at Mary Beth when she reached his side. Taylor ignored her.

"I thought you were at the shore, Taylor," he said.

"After you cancelled," she pouted, "our other guests did too. Daddy, Mum, and I decided to stay home and see what the locals do."

Her perfectly made-up face brightened. "We're having a little party at our house after the fireworks." She stared up at Tom, her eyes wide. "Please join us," she purred.

Taylor's words and her proprietary attitude toward Tom made Mary Beth tighten her lips and curl her fingers into her palms.

Tom freed himself from Taylor and reached out to put his arm around Mary Beth's waist and draw her close.

Immobilized by surprise, Mary Beth stood stiffly in his protective embrace. The realization that he had pulled her to him in front of Taylor sent happiness surging through her. She relaxed against him.

"We have plans afterward," he said.

Mary Beth sent him a glance, but his expression was unreadable. If he wanted to use her to get out of an evening with the Bennetts, she'd let him.

Taylor's contemptuous gaze swept over Mary Beth. Mary Beth arched an eyebrow and stared back.

"Tom, can I see you for a minute?" Taylor's father, standing with some men a few feet away, beckoned.

"Be right back," Tom said to Mary Beth. He headed for the group.

"So you two are having another fling," Taylor said when they were alone. Her tight voice and ice blue gaze sent chills through Mary Beth.

"That's really none of your business, Taylor."

The blond moved closer. The malice in her eyes made Mary Beth want to take a step back, but she held her ground.

"Don't get too sure of yourself," Taylor hissed. "Tom's just with you because you're different. Once he has his fill of you, he'll be back where he belongs. With his own kind. With me."

Mary Beth stretched herself up to her full height and stared into the woman's cold eyes. "Grow up, Taylor," she said.

Throwing her a look dripping with venom, the blond stalked away.

"Everything okay?" Tom asked, coming up to Mary Beth.

She moved closer to him. "It is now," she said.

* * *

With the blanket slung casually over his shoulder, Tom grabbed Mary Beth's hand. They followed the crowd out of the darkened park. The swell of people forced her to stay close to him.

Wrapped in a sweet cocoon with Tom, she barely noticed the cries of small children and the talk and laughter that swirled around them.

The feel of his lean, muscular body sent delicious shivers through her. She wanted his closeness, wanted her hand in his. She'd enjoyed being with him tonight. He always made her feel more alive, all her senses sharpened.

Mary Beth inhaled the acrid smell of the lingering fireworks mixing with the flower-laced air. The whole evening had been like that, the bitter with the sweet.

Her conversation with Taylor had left a bad taste in her mouth. But that didn't matter now. Tom walked beside her.

Over the past months, and especially hours ago in her apartment, he had peeled away layers of himself, revealing a kind, sensitive man, so different from the Tom simmering in her memories all these years. At the park tonight he'd been so attentive, particularly in front of Taylor. Mary Beth's pride had slowly melted with each new layer he exposed.

She glanced up at his strong profile. The truth hit her like a bucket of ice water. She needed Tom Sackett. Needed his strength and his acceptance of the woman she'd become and not of her as his teenage fantasy. Longing, and a dash of fear, stirred a heady brew in her stomach.

Someone in the crowd bumped hard against her, making her gasp.

Tom shifted the blanket to his other shoulder and tightened his grip on her hand. "Let's get out of here before you're trampled," he said.

She nodded, warmed by the concern in his voice.

He pulled her through the crowd, clearing a path for her, protecting her.

It had been so long since anyone took care of her, since anyone made her feel special. Her last residue of doubt dissolved into the warm summer night.

"This is better," Tom said when they'd reached a moon-dappled side street. A few pedestrians hurried by.

He slipped his arm around her waist and drew her closer. She leaned her head against the hard muscles of his upper arm and breathed in his unique scent of light citrus and heated masculinity.

"I liked the way the crowd kept pushing you against me," he drawled. "They didn't give you a chance to pull away like you always do."

"I'm not pulling away now," she said, glancing up at him.

"So you're not," he said. His penetrating gaze made her insides shake.

He stopped and turned her to face him. With his thumb and forefinger, he lifted her chin to look into her eyes.

"I had fun tonight," he said quietly. "I like being with you."

She swallowed. "I had fun too."

"You're not afraid anymore?" His gaze searched hers.

"I don't know, Tom. I really don't know." A small grain of fear lodged in her throat. Could she trust him?

He brushed his finger slowly over her mouth. She shivered and parted her lips.

He slid his hand down her arm. The roughness of his skin against hers made warmth spread over her.

"It's a long way back to your apartment," he said. "I think we could both use the walk."

Disappointment and embarrassment sliced through her. She'd been practically panting for him to kiss her.

When they reached the old Victorian, she faced him, prepared to say good-bye. Years of tightly reined emotions warred with her yearning for him. If he left now she'd be safe. Did she want safe?

"I'll walk you up to your apartment," he said.

"You don't. . . ."

"No arguments," he whispered. He touched his finger to her lips, stopping any further protests.

Tom cupped her elbow as he followed her up the steep stairs. His touch scorched her, making her grip the railing for support.

When they reached her apartment, she unlocked the door, then turned to him.

"Thanks for everything," she said. Her voice sounded thin. "It's late. I'd better go."

"You're not going to invite me in for coffee?" he said.

The closeness they'd shared all evening held her as firmly as his burning gaze. The past didn't matter. Nor the future. There was only now.

"You trust yourself alone with me?" she said.

His smile made her heart skip a beat. "No," he said. "But I can handle it."

She pushed her apartment door open. He followed her, closing the door behind him.

"Mary Beth," he said in a gruff voice.

She turned to him, lifting her face to his. He gathered her into his arms. The blanket slipped off his shoulder to brush her body as it slid to the floor. The soft wool felt harsh against her heated skin.

Tom kissed her with an urgency that seared her. She wound her arms around his neck and returned his kiss, giving him her heart and her soul.

He reached behind her to unbraid her hair. The heaviness of the curls cascaded down her back and over her shoulders.

He released her to cup her face between his hands. "You are so beautiful," he whispered. He slid his fingers through her hair, a reverent look on his face. "I've dreamed of you like this."

She refused to admit, even to herself, that she'd dreamed of him too. "Tom," she breathed, reaching out her hand to trace the curve of his lips.

He pulled her to him and buried his face in her hair. "So sweet," he murmured. "So soft."

She clung to him, raining light kisses on his neck, inhaling his warm scent of summer-laced breezes. Happiness sang through her veins. The tenderness of his touch slowly dissolved the old hurts. She melted against him, pliant in his arms.

She took his face between her hands and kissed him, wanting to savor his taste. Cupping the back of her head, he moved his lips slowly over hers.

The truth snaked its way into her consciousness, wrapping around her heart until she could no longer ignore it. She loved Tom. Had always loved him. And always would. But the joy of being in his arms was tempered with anxiety. Would he abandon her again?

Tom pulled away and stared at her. He rubbed his thumb over her cheekbone. "You've been my fantasy for years, Cat Eyes."

She stiffened. The golden glow that filled her dissipated, leaving her hollow inside.

"I'm not a fantasy, Tom. I'm real."

"Very real," he whispered, drawing her closer. "Mary Beth, you are so different from anyone I've ever known."

His words froze her. Her old insecurities rushed at her, knocking her with hurricane-force winds.

Like an evil storm, Taylor's words hovered over them. *Once he has his fill of you, he'll be back where he belongs.* She hated to think the icy blond was right.

Her body shook. She pushed away. She couldn't do it. Couldn't allow him into her heart. Her feelings for Tom were deeper, more mature than before. If he rejected her again, the pain would push so deep she would never heal.

Tears threatened to spill. She wanted him to love *her,* Mary Beth Kendrick, not a dream he'd conjured up in his head these past years. Reality seldom lived up to fantasy. How long before Tom tired of her?

She lifted her chin. He wouldn't get the chance to desert her. This time she was in control.

"Mary Beth?" He frowned, a questioning look on his face.

Cold resolve stiffened her spine. What a fool to dream Tom could love her, that they had a future together. They were from different worlds and always would be.

"You'd better go, Tom," she said in a tight voice. Her heart seemed to shatter like delicate crystal thrown against marble, but she held herself rigid, hiding her despair.

"What?" Shock hardened his features. Disbelief flickered in the blue depths of his eyes. She fought the temptation to caress his face, to tell him she loved him. Pride, her defense for so many years, held her.

He touched her chin. She flinched.

"Mary Beth, what's going on? Don't shut me out."

His gentle voice seduced her. She bit down on her lip.

To send him away now would leave a dull ache in her. But to lose herself to him only to have him toss her aside later would sear her with a burning pain that would last forever.

She breathed deeply, mustering her courage. "There can never be anything but business between us." She moved away, folding her arms across her chest, as if she could protect herself from the heartbreak that emptied her soul.

Tom combed his fingers through his thick hair. Tension creased his forehead.

"I thought we had an understanding," he said. "We have something, Mary Beth. Don't throw it away. Talk to me."

Once he's had his fill of you, he'll leave. The mocking words played over and over in her head. She dug her nails into her palms. "Go, please. Don't make this any more difficult."

Anger replaced the confusion on Tom's face. His eyes narrowed to dark slits.

"I need an explanation," he said tersely.

She chewed her lip. "The fireworks, the good time we had, lulled me into forgetting, but I've come to my senses now."

"Forgetting what?" he said in disbelief. He moved toward her. She backed away. He stopped. They stood in the middle of the room, facing each other. Tension covered them like a thick blanket.

"I'm not interested in anything other than a business relationship with you," she said. The lie wedged into her heart like a sharp knife.

Hurt shadowed his eyes. She wanted to go to him. But she couldn't release her heart. Too much pride and too much pain stood between them.

He let his breath out. Resignation softened his features.

"I guess I was wrong about you. You're not the Mary Beth I used to know. I won't bother you again."

Pain flitted across his sculpted features before he turned to stride quickly out of the room. The loud click of her apartment door locking behind him left Mary Beth feeling utterly alone.

She sank slowly down onto the hard wooden floor. She choked back tears and hugged herself.

"What have I done?" she whispered.

Chapter Nine

C r-a-a-ck! Mary Beth jumped at the sound of the auctioneer's gavel striking wood. She slid a glance at the men and women, business owners like herself, who waited backstage with her for the charity auction to begin.

The others seemed oblivious to the tension in the air as they chatted and drank champagne cocktails. Was she the only one who felt like a rolled-up flank steak to be sold to the highest bidder?

She pulled at the plunging neckline of her tight-fitting gown and fanned herself with the program she held. Whatever had possessed her to wear satin in August? And how had she let Gail talk her into this?

The rustle of the audience taking their seats made sweat form on her palms. She swallowed and looked around for Gail. As co-chair of the prestigious event,

Gail had flitted around all day like a butterfly on steroids. She caught Gail slipping through the heavy curtains from the front of the theater and beckoned to her.

"I can't do this," Mary Beth said when Gail reached her.

"Of course you can," Gail said. "Just relax and let yourself have fun for a change. Think about all the money we'll raise for the kids."

Mary Beth blew her breath out. "I'm glad to help the kids, but there must be another way that doesn't involve my being put on the auction block."

"You are not being auctioned off," Gail said, reaching out a hand to tuck a trailing wisp of hair back into Mary Beth's chignon. "The bid is for your services as a chef. And you look great. So don't worry."

"Ladies and gentlemen," barked the auctioneer. "The third annual auction to benefit the Kids AIDS Foundation is about to begin."

"Oh, God," Mary Beth whispered. She gave Gail a nervous look and started to take her place in line with the other participants.

Gail's hand on her arm stopped her. "There's something I have to tell you." She took a deep breath. "Tom's in the audience. With Taylor. But they didn't arrive together. I saw her push herself on him."

Mary Beth's heart knocked against her chest. In a daze, she filed onto the stage with the others and took her seat.

Since she sent Tom away four weeks ago, she'd seen him a handful of times at business meetings. He always treated her with cool politeness, nothing more. Pride told her she'd made the right decision, but the ache in her heart grew sharper every day.

Against her will, she scanned the elegantly clad crowd. Her stomach tightened when she spotted Tom in the second row. Like most men, he looked handsome in a tux, but Tom's sculpted looks made him stand out from the other well-dressed men. She swallowed the dryness in her throat.

His gaze caught and held hers. She couldn't look away. Taylor, cool and elegant in black and diamonds, whispered in his ear, drawing his attention away.

Crack! The auctioneer's gavel echoed the breaking of Mary Beth's heart.

The auction got underway amid raucous shouts and laughter. Mary Beth tried to smile, but her lips trembled. She clasped her hands on her lap.

One after another of the services offered went to the highest bidder until only she and elderly Mrs. Bloom of Bloom's Blossoms remained. Mary Beth forced a smile. Soon it would all be over.

"Our next item is a gourmet meal for two cooked in your home by one of the city's best chefs, Mary Beth Kendrick, of Kendrick and Company Caterers and Party Planners," the auctioneer shouted. "This is a real treat, folks. Do I have a bid?"

"Two hundred dollars," a male voice rang out.

Widening her eyes, Mary Beth stared in the direction of the voice. A brown-haired young attorney she had met at a recent party smiled at her. She gulped.

Other bids, in small increments, were yelled out.

"Ladies and gentlemen, you can do better than that," snapped the auctioneer. "It's for a good cause and I hear this little redhead's cooking is as delectable as she is."

Mary Beth wanted to sink lower in her chair, but she kept the smile plastered on her face.

"Six hundred dollars." The attorney again.

"That's more like it," said the auctioneer. "Come on. You ladies too. Ms. Kendrick will cook up a romantic dinner for you and the man in your life. Maybe he'll even pop the question."

Laughter, then several women shouted bids.

"Fifteen hundred dollars." Tom's voice rang out above the rest. A collective gasp rose up from the audience.

Please, God. No, Mary Beth pleaded. She met Tom's gaze. The heat in his eyes sent a sizzling warmth coursing through her.

"Seventeen hundred." The attorney.

"Now we're cooking," bellowed the auctioneer.

"Thirty-five hundred." Tom.

Ripples of excitement swept through the crowd. Mary Beth's cheeks burned. She must look like a Christmas decoration. Bright red skin against the green of her dress.

She slid a glance toward Taylor. With a frantic look on her face, the other woman leaned over to whisper to Tom. Mary Beth hadn't thought it possible that the blond could get any paler, but her white features made fresh snow look like an artist's palette.

"Any more bids?" yelled the auctioneer. "Going once. . . ."

"Four thousand." The attorney.

"Six thousand." Tom.

A hush settled over the audience. Tension throbbed like a palpable force. Mary Beth's mind shut down.

"Six thousand dollars. Going once. Going twice. Sold to the gentleman in the second row."

The auctioneer's excited voice and the crowd's enthusiastic applause penetrated the fog in Mary Beth's brain. Like an accident victim in shock, she turned her head slowly in Tom's direction.

Taylor jumped up, and with a toss of her head, stormed out. Tom stared at Mary Beth, a challenge in his dark gaze.

Mary Beth balled her hands to stop their shaking. Did anyone really believe that Tom paid six thousand dollars just for dinner?

Men! Mary Beth pulled the asparagus steamer out of her bag and plunked it down on the black granite counter in Tom's kitchen. It voiced its protest with a loud clang. Knife in hand, she began trimming the thick ends off the vegetables she had set out earlier.

Darn Tom! Embarrassing her in front of all those people at the auction two weeks ago. She chopped faster. And today his housekeeper mentioned he had a special lady coming for dinner. What a way to spend

Saturday night, cooking for Tom and a date. Would it be Taylor? Or someone new?

Pain, sharp as the instrument she held, sliced into her at the picture of Tom with another woman. She lopped the end off the last stalk with enough force to scratch the plastic cutting board.

Mary Beth lay the knife down before she cut herself and shoved away from the counter. Jamming her hands in her apron pockets, she turned to face Tom's spacious kitchen, done in shades of black, gray, and white.

What other women had he brought into his kitchen, into his house? "No," she said, shaking her head. Thoughts like that weakened her. She had to stay angry. Anger kept the heartache at bay.

Straightening, she headed toward the refrigerator. She had a six-thousand-dollar meal to prepare.

What had Tom been thinking? Six thousand dollars for dinner? Had he meant to embarrass her or had his competitive nature kicked in? The Tom she used to know needed to win, at all costs. Maybe he hadn't changed after all.

Focus on the food, she told herself as she yanked open the stainless steel door of the refrigerator. Her gaze swept over the shelves she had stocked that afternoon. Paper-thin slices of smoked salmon and the finest Russian caviar cooled in crystal bowls covered with plastic wrap.

The cinnamon scent of Gail's apple crisp made her mouth water. She'd bake the rich concoction in delicate pastry shells. Homemade cinnamon ice cream waited in the freezer, a delicious accompaniment to the baked dessert.

She grabbed the bag of mixed greens and tossed it on the counter next to the raspberry vinaigrette ingredients. Wiping her hands on a towel, she glanced out the bay window. Dark already. Tom would be home from work soon—called out on an emergency, his housekeeper had said. Would he have his date with him?

Mary Beth pushed the refrigerator door shut and leaned against it, closing her eyes. The pain of missing Tom all these weeks and knowing that he would be with another woman tonight seared through her.

Fingering the gold chain around her neck like a calming talisman, she stared across the room to where stainless steel pots hung from a rack. She had steel in her too and she would get through this night.

With her shoulders squared, she strode across the tiled floor to the oven and pulled open the door. The succulent odor of orange duck greeted her. Almost done. The brioche would go in soon and then. . . .

"Hello, Mary Beth." Tom's deep voice rang out behind her.

She jumped back. The oven door slammed shut. Taking a deep breath, she turned to face him.

"I hope that's not a soufflé in there," he said.

"It's not." She hated that her voice sounded thin.

"Whatever it is, it smells delicious." Tom stood just inside the doorway, his thumbs hooked in the pockets of his jeans, his black T-shirt stretching over the broadness of his chest. She dug her nails into her palms, fighting her weakness for him.

"Must you always sneak up on me?" she said, dredging up her anger.

He raked his fingers through his thick hair. "I see your attitude hasn't improved over the past weeks."

"What's that supposed to mean?" She put her hand on her hip and glared at him.

They stared at each other. The rigid set of his shoulders mirrored her tension.

"Forget it," he said.

"Where's your date?" she asked, forcing coolness into her voice.

"Date?" He arched an eyebrow.

"I thought. . . ." She raised her chin. "You bid on dinner for two."

His blue eyes searched hers. "So I did. Don't concern yourself with my date."

Anger and hurt mixed in her stomach. "I am not concerned with your date. Dinner's almost ready. If you know anything about cooking, timing is everything."

He stepped close, dangerously close. She inhaled the woodsy, masculine scent of the outdoors that clung to him. Her breathing quickened.

"Was the timing off between us?" he said in a low voice. "Is that the problem?"

She resisted the impulse to back away from him and the temptation he offered. "I don't know what you're talking about. I just want to finish this meal and leave."

He cupped her chin in his hand. "You know exactly what I'm talking about."

The heat of his touch filled her with longing. She jerked free.

"You don't trust me," he said. "Or maybe you don't trust yourself."

The truth of his words hit her. She pressed against the counter and crossed her arms. "You made a spectacle of me at the auction," she said, anxious to change the subject. "Bidding an outrageous sum for dinner. No one in the audience believed you paid six thousand dollars just for my cooking."

A muscle worked in his jaw. "I attended that auction for only one reason. And I got what I wanted."

"What was that?" The question slipped from her.

"What do you think I wanted?" he growled.

She met his fiery gaze. "I'm not sure," she said, angling her chin. "To publicly humiliate me?"

"Humiliate you? What do you take me for?"

She flinched at the bitterness in his voice and slid her gaze away from his.

He reached out to wrap his hand around her braid and turn her face toward him. "I wanted to have dinner with you." His voice was harsh. "I needed to talk to you. But every time I saw you it was strictly business."

"Dinner?" she said, swallowing. "You paid six thousand dollars to have dinner with me?"

"Yes, crazy as it sounds."

She locked her gaze with his, looking to confirm the honesty of his words, startled by what she saw there. Yearning sliced through her.

"You could have told me," she said. "I don't appreciate being used." She couldn't stop the huskiness that seeped into her voice. The light in his blue eyes showed that he heard it too.

"Used? I would never use you." Despite his words, his tone had softened. He cupped the back of her neck. "I could say you used me, Cat Eyes."

At her quick intake of breath, he put his finger over her lips. "But you wouldn't do that to me. I know you better than that. What happened, Mary Beth?"

"Nothing," she said, averting her gaze from the deep blue of his eyes, eyes that demanded an answer.

He touched her chin, making her look at him. She knew she should pull away but she wanted his nearness.

"Something is going on," he said. "I thought we were friends. More than friends."

"We're in business together," she said, shaking her head. "Nothing more. It can't be anything more." No matter how rebellious her heart, she wouldn't succumb.

"Why can't there be anything more between us?" he asked quietly. "I've missed you, Cat Eyes. I couldn't stay away."

He lowered his head to meet her lips in a kiss that told her the truth of his words. She put her hands on his chest and stood stiffly in his arms, trying to hold onto her last crumbs of pride. But her own desires and his tenderness turned her bones to butter. She swayed against him.

The timer shrilled. The high-pitched tone jarred her. She pulled away. They stared at each other. His ragged breathing matched hers. With a trembling hand, she pushed a stray curl off her forehead.

The timer continued to pierce the charged atmosphere. "Darn," Tom muttered.

He left her to stride across the room. She hugged herself, missing the security of his arms.

He turned off the timer and the oven with quick flicks of his wrist. Reality filled her with uncertainties. The echoes of Taylor's bitter prediction twisted like a knife inside her. She scooted to the far end of the counter.

"This is not about missing me," she said, clutching at her last shred of dignity. "This is simply because you hate to lose anything, or anyone."

He turned and faced her. His harsh expression and the firm set of his jaw hinted at tightly controlled emotions. She chewed her lip, unable to take her gaze from his.

"There's nothing simple about anything between us, Mary Beth. And I grew out of my need to win a long time ago."

"Really?" she said, arching an eyebrow. "You don't call a bidding war at the auction competitive?"

"The prize was worth the fight," he said.

She swallowed. "I'm just a commodity, then?"

Lines of fatigue and frustration bracketed his mouth. "That's not what I meant, and you know it."

She folded her arms over her chest, sure he could hear the wild beating of her heart across the expanse of kitchen.

He walked slowly toward her. She backed into the counter.

"What will it take for you to believe me?" he said in a tortured voice.

"Believe what?" she whispered.

He slid his hands down her arms. His touch sent excitement skittering up her spine.

"Believe that I want to be with you," he replied huskily. "That I miss you when you're not around."

Her fears began to slowly evaporate under his searching gaze.

"I–I want to believe you, Tom," she said, lowering her gaze. "But I'm afraid." Her admission shook her. She had to be more careful. She couldn't let him know what her heart desired.

"Afraid of what, Mary Beth? Look at me."

She looked deep into his eyes and knew that she couldn't stop loving him any more than she could stop breathing. She shivered.

"You haven't answered me," he said. He tightened his grip on her arms. "What are you afraid of?"

"Please don't ask me that," she said. "I'm not ready to talk about it."

He released her arms and raked his fingers through

his hair. "You are the most frustrating and stubborn woman I've ever met," he said.

He grabbed her shoulders and pulled her closer. "I won't pressure you," he said. "I'm willing to wait until you're ready to tell me what's in that beautiful head of yours. I want to see you. And not just during business hours."

The alarm bells in her head threatened to deafen her. He hadn't said he loved her or made any promises. How long before she ceased to be a challenge? And could she survive losing him a second time?

She locked her gaze with his. She was strong. She would handle whatever happened between them. Anxiety gripped her, but she pushed it away. She loved him so much and she wanted to be with him, even if only for a little while.

"I–I want to see you too," she whispered.

Relief washed over his features. He gathered her to him. Delicious shivers sped along her nerve endings.

"My Cat Eyes," he whispered.

She barely noticed his fingers in her hair until she felt its thickness tumble over her shoulders. He dipped his head to brush her lips in a kiss that poured out his longings.

She returned his kiss, ignoring the small voice of reason that seasoned her happiness with apprehension.

Chapter Ten

"What is going on with you and Tom?"

Mary Beth dropped the paper towel she was using to clean the counter in the catering shop kitchen and swung around to face Gail. "What do you mean?"

Eyes narrowed and arms folded across her chest in a "take no prisoners" stance, Gail glared at her. "I'm worried about you and I want to know what the deal is between you two. You've been seeing each other since August and it's now October. Tom never takes you out. It's either his place or yours. Is he ashamed of you? Does he think he's better than you just because he's rich?" Gail's nostrils flared in indignation.

Tension knotted Mary Beth's stomach. She bit down on her lip. The ecstasy of being with Tom these weeks was tempered by the fear that he would leave her again. Gail continued to stare, an expectant look on her face.

"It's something like that," Mary Beth said.

"That rat!" Anger sparked in Gail's eyes. "To think I liked him. I even pushed you two together."

"Simmer down," Mary Beth said, holding up her hand. "You've got it wrong." She blew her breath out. "Partially wrong anyway."

Gail combed her fingers through her unruly curls. "Pulling taffy is easier than pulling anything out of you," she said.

"Don't you have to go home?" Mary Beth glanced at the clock. "Isn't your family waiting for dinner?"

"I'm not budging till you explain," Gail said, jutting out her jaw.

"There's nothing to explain," Mary Beth said. She could barely acknowledge her uncertainties to herself, let alone share them with someone else.

"Darn it, Mary Beth. You're my best friend. My partner. I don't want you hurt. You look as tightly corked as an unopened bottle of wine. If Tom's ashamed of you, dump him. You're too good for him."

Mary Beth took a deep breath and leveled her gaze at Gail. "Don't be hard on Tom. I'm the one who doesn't want anyone to know we're together."

"What?" Gail's gray eyes widened. "I've got to sit." She pulled out a stool and plopped down. "Have you gone completely bonkers? It's obvious you're in love with Tom. Why hide it?"

Mary Beth tugged on her braid. "Because he's not in love with me," she said. She swallowed around the lump in her throat.

"How do you know he doesn't love you?" Gail asked. "It's hard for some men to say the words."

"I know," Mary Beth said. "He calls me his fantasy. His Cat Eyes. He's playing out our unfinished business from high school."

Mary Beth glanced across the room to the windows. Shades covered the darkness outside, just as her heart had closed against intimacy for so many years. She'd opened a little to let Tom in again, and she'd pay the price. Sadness swept over her.

"Have you told Tom you love him?" Gail asked.

Mary Beth turned to her friend. "I told him once. Long ago. And look what happened. To Tom I'm still the girl from the wrong part of town. The girl who's different. Once I cease to excite him, he'll go back where he belongs. They always go back where they belong." She couldn't keep the bitterness from seeping into her voice.

"Have you ever talked to him about that incident at the formal?" Gail's gaze locked with hers.

Mary Beth shook her head.

"Why not?" Gail said.

Chewing her lip, Mary Beth turned her gaze from her friend's accusing stare. Old hurts simmered in her, threatening to bubble over. She pressed against the counter edge.

Angling her chin, she faced Gail. "I learned many

years ago that some things are best left alone. If you bring them out, they'll just hurt you all over again."

Gail's expression softened and she slid off the stool to approach Mary Beth. "Oh, honey, you've got it all wrong. You need to talk to him."

"No, I can't," Mary Beth said. "I wish I could open up to him, but I'm afraid of what I'll dredge up."

The jingle of the front doorbell intruded. Mary Beth let her breath out, relieved to put an end to their conversation. She didn't want to talk about Tom. She still hadn't sorted out her relationship with him in her own mind.

Gail touched her hand. "I'll get it."

"Hi, Tom." Gail's words rang out from the other room. "She's in the back."

"Thanks, Gail."

At the sound of Tom's deep voice, Mary Beth's heart seemed to take a flying leap out of her chest. She turned toward the kitchen doorway.

Tom sauntered in. A smile curved his lips when he saw Mary Beth. They stared at each other, the atmosphere charged between them. She feasted on him with her hungry gaze. He took her breath away with his beauty. His dark blue suit enhanced the deep color of his eyes. With his white shirt unbuttoned at the top and his tie loosened, he looked incredibly alluring. She wanted to devour him.

Gail followed him into the room. She gave Mary Beth a pointed look. "If you two don't mind, I have to leave," she said, grabbing her jacket and purse from the hook on the wall. Mary Beth thought she mumbled good-bye to Gail, but Tom's nearness clouded her mind.

"Hi, Cat Eyes," he said. He walked slowly toward her, his body moving with the easy grace she knew so well. She barely noticed the sound of the outside door shutting behind Gail.

He stood close. Her insides quivered like half-baked soufflé. She inhaled the faint citrus of his cologne. Her bones seemed to dissolve.

Tom took her chin between his fingers and lowered his head to brush his lips over hers.

Standing on her toes, she wound her arms around his neck. His kiss sent delicious shivers dancing along her skin. She savored his taste of coffee and mint.

He drew his mouth away from hers and held her close. His warm breath teased her neck.

"I missed you," he said.

She laughed softly. "We saw each other just last night."

He pulled away and slid his hands down her arms. "Whenever you're not with me I miss you," he said. "You are the most intriguing woman I've ever known."

At his hint of other women, tendrils of jealousy pulled at her heart. She forced the feeling away. Tom was here now, with her. The past and the future didn't matter.

"You are the most beautiful man I've ever known," she said, forcing lightness into her voice. Tom always made her feel special, but he never said he loved her. She couldn't let him know how much he meant to her.

He gathered her to him and brushed a feather-soft kiss on her temple. His tenderness warmed her with a bittersweet yearning.

"I sat in on a budget meeting most of the afternoon," he said. "But I couldn't concentrate. All I could think about was you. Seeing you. Being with you." His husky voice held her as securely as his strong arms. "It's a good thing my family owns the company or I'd be out of a job. You've cast a spell on me."

She laid her head against his hard chest and breathed in his unique masculine scent mixed with the faint hint of wool and starched cotton. Longing, mixed with sadness, coursed through her. She loved him so much. If only he loved her too.

His hands bracketed her waist and he drew back to stare down at her. "Let's go out to dinner for a change. Gretchen's in Greenville makes the best pizza, and their patio is still open."

Tension stiffened her spine. Thursday was the big night for the trendy eatery. Half the city would be there. The more people who knew about her and Tom, the more witnesses to her heartbreak when their relationship ended.

She freed herself and slid her gaze away from his. "I just have to put some things away and I'll be ready," she said.

Trying to collect her thoughts, she grabbed the bag

of carrots from the counter and walked to the refrigerator.

"Why don't we go back to your place," she said, opening the refrigerator and dropping the vegetables on a shelf.

She closed the door and leaned against it, tossing a glance toward Tom. "We can order pizza from Ernesto's," she said. "It's almost as good as Gretchen's and we don't have to go out."

"Darn it, Mary Beth." Frustration filled Tom's voice. Loosening his tie, he moved closer. "What's the problem?" He stood inches from her. A muscle worked in his jaw.

She wanted to shrink from his anger. She straightened and met his gaze.

"Every time I mention going out," he said, "you find an excuse to stay in." He ran his hand over his hair and moved away to pace the kitchen like an angry panther.

She narrowed her eyes and watched him. Why was he so upset? They spent lots of time together. Why should he care if they went out?

He stopped his pacing and pivoted to face her across the room. His features were harsh and his mouth set in a grim line. "Am I such a horrible person that you're afraid to be seen with me? Are you hiding from someone? Is there another man?"

The fear that flickered in his eyes made her heart twist with hope. A false hope that would only hurt her in the end. She blinked back tears.

"That's not it, Tom. None of those things."

"Then what's wrong?"

She flinched but stood her ground. They stared at each other. Tension arced between them.

She looked down at the floor. She couldn't tell him the truth and admit her fears. And her love. The habits of a lifetime that had protected her heart all these years wouldn't break.

He let out a sigh. "Okay. I'll give in to you. Again. But I want you to go to the Harvest Ball with me."

She jerked her gaze back to him and shook her head. "I can't," she said, fingering the gold chain at her neck. "You know I have to work the ball. It's our biggest job so far and I can't leave Gail to do it alone."

He set his jaw in a stubborn line. She braced herself for the storm to come.

"And you know that Gail can hire all the help she needs. She'll be fine without you." His quiet, deliberate tone told her the effort it cost for him to control his anger. She pressed against the cold stainless steel of the refrigerator.

With tension in every line of his lean body, Tom moved slowly closer. She thrust her chin out, ready to do battle. The Harvest Ball benefited several prestigious private schools, including St. Anselm's. Many of their old classmates would be there. No way would she put herself on display by attending with Tom.

"Talk to me, Mary Beth." His blue gaze searched hers. "Tell me what's going on behind those green cat eyes."

"I can't."

"Can't? Or won't?" he said in a tight voice.

Tom wrapped his hand around her braid, tipping back her head. "You always seem happy to see me. But you won't go out in public with me. What kind of game are you playing?"

He meant so much to her, but she couldn't tell him. She knew when this was over she'd be shattered, but she couldn't bear his pity when the inevitable happened.

She placed her hand on his chest. His heart beat fast and strong through the soft wool of his jacket.

"I'm not playing games, Tom. I swear. It's not what you think." Her need for him was real, filling her waking hours and peppering her dreams. She loved his smile, his easy laugh, and the sparkle in his deep blue eyes. She sensed a depth to him, a caring nature that he tried to hide under the fun and the laughter.

He wasn't hers to keep. If she couldn't have him forever, she would take whatever he offered now. Pain twisted in her.

He grabbed her hands in his. "What is it? You don't trust me enough to open up to me." Hurt flickered in his eyes.

"I can't talk about it," she said.

He put his hands on the refrigerator over her shoulders. Frustration flashed over his chiseled features.

"Tell me what's wrong, Mary Beth. I'm proud to be seen with you. I want the whole world to know about us."

"Tom, let's just enjoy being together. Please don't ask me things I can't talk about."

She took his face between her hands and reached up to kiss him with the longing she couldn't confess. He placed his mouth hard over hers, making her pulse race.

Releasing her, he folded her into his embrace. "You're mine, Cat Eyes," he whispered.

But for how long? she thought. She curled her arms around his neck, clinging to him. She never wanted to let him go.

Chapter Eleven

"I have to hang up now, Mary Beth." Her mother's happy voice hummed over the telephone wires. "I have a golf lesson, then I'm meeting Victor for dinner. Such a nice man."

"Wait, Mom. Don't. . . ." Dial tone replaced her mother's babbling. Stomach shaking, Mary Beth slowly hung up the phone and sank into the thick cushions of her sofa.

"Wow," she said to the empty room. "I didn't see that one coming."

She'd had enough stress in the last two days just dealing with Tom. Despite her protests, he wouldn't let up his pressure on her to attend the Harvest Ball with him.

Now this. Her mother's decision to stay in Arizona permanently with Aunt Linda was shock enough. But

Dorothy Kendrick learning to play golf? Working for a florist in Phoenix? Dating a man? Mary Beth's head spun.

She stared around her quiet living room as tears filled her eyes. Her mother didn't need her anymore. She, Mary Beth Kendrick, was completely on her own for the first time in her life.

"Get over it, Mary Beth," she said, running her fingers through her hair, still damp from the shower. The familiar gesture couldn't ease the loneliness that had taken root.

Her mom had been a challenge for so many years. She should be relieved to see her happily settled somewhere else. So why did she feel as if a huge chunk of her life had been torn off and thrown away like a bad piece of meat?

Sadness knotted her stomach. She grabbed a small pillow from the couch and hugged it. Tom didn't need her either. At least not permanently.

Her world had changed the day Tom returned. Her ailing business was healthy again. Soon she and Gail could afford to buy their company back from Sackett Industries.

Despite Tom's hurtful actions all those years ago, he'd been good to her these last months. Had he been trying to make amends? Would he bail out once he felt he'd paid his debt to her? Bile rose in her throat. She wanted his love, not his pity.

Rubbing her aching temples, she leaned her head back and closed her eyes. Images from her past played out in her mind like an old movie. The laughter and happiness when her family was intact. The terrible hurt and loneliness when her dad walked out on them. Her mother's steadfast refusal to allow Mary Beth to talk about her father.

She wiped away a tear. Tom's betrayal at the formal had reinforced what her mother had always taught her. Men couldn't be trusted. They always left in the end.

Yet her mom, whose wounds cut so deep, had summoned the courage to shake the pain at last and open up to life again. Could she do the same?

Unable to sit still, she got up to pace the room, trying to digest the mix of emotions coursing through her. Stopping in front of a low table, she picked up a small snow globe—a gift from her dad just before he deserted them. She turned the toy over and watched the flakes fall over the smiling figures sledding down a slope.

She stared at the happy family encased forever in glass, then opened the table drawer and tucked the globe inside, closing the drawer tight. The past was over. It wouldn't hurt her anymore.

Wind rattled the windows. Leaves swirled by on the strong gusts. Like the trees, she had to shed her old insecurities to make room for a new beginning.

And Tom? Where did he fit in? She loved him deeply, but was she brave enough to set aside her fears to love him openly and freely regardless of the consequences? The Harvest Ball meant a lot to him. And he meant the world to her.

Tension sliced through her, but she pushed it away. She would do this. For Tom. For herself. She picked up the phone and punched in the familiar number. "Hi, Tom," she said when he answered. "I'm calling because. . . ." She took a deep breath. "I've reconsidered, and if your offer still stands, I'd be happy to go to the Harvest Ball with you."

"Wow!" Tom said when Mary Beth opened her apartment door. He let out a low whistle.

He closed the door behind him and leaned against it, staring at her. The form-fitting satin gown, green as her eyes, hugged her lush curves. Her beauty stole his breath away.

She smiled, that dazzling smile that always made his heart skip a beat. His Mary Beth. Smart, proud, passionate. Possessiveness, and a new emotion, a realization long denied, clutched his gut. He wanted her—needed her—by his side. Forever.

"I take it you like," Mary Beth said. She did a slow pirouette.

"I like very much," he said, finding his voice. "You're beautiful."

Her happy laugh sent warmth coursing through him.

He devoured her with his gaze. "You wore that to the auction. The color matches your eyes."

Feeling like a bumbling idiot, he stepped closer. She stared up at him with those slanted cat eyes that could make him forget his name.

He reached out a trembling hand to trail his finger

along her jawline. Could she read the truth in his eyes? Did she feel the same way? Afraid of the answer, he couldn't ask the question.

Her low laugh tinkled through the room like crystal. "You look amazing in a tux." She ran her fingers slowly down his lapels.

He pulled her to him. He inhaled her perfume, musky and exotic. Different from the flowery scents she usually wore. Despite her reluctance to attend the Harvest Ball, she'd taken care to make this night special. For him? A glimmer of hope opened in his heart.

He lowered his head to kiss her. She tasted sweet, like cinnamon and apples. She melted against him, lacing her arms around his neck.

With an effort he pulled away. She let out a small cry. Strands of curls had loosened from her elegant hairstyle. She looked wild, like a gypsy. His heart lurched.

He leaned his forehead against hers. He wanted to claim her as his, but he'd been hurt once. Despite their closeness these past months, Mary Beth held part of herself back.

"I could kiss you for hours," he whispered. "But we're not missing this party. I want to show you off, to let everyone know you're mine." Was it his imagination, or did she stiffen slightly?

He traced his finger over her delicious lips. "Someday, Cat Eyes, you're going to trust me enough to let me in."

Something close to fear flickered in the glistening

green of her eyes. She drew away. "I'll get my wrap," she said.

"In a minute." He took her hand and kissed it, smoothing his fingers over the silver bracelet she wore. A small heart dangled from the delicate links. "What's this?" he said. "It looks familiar."

Pink tinged her cheeks. "You gave me this our junior year after I tutored you. I haven't worn it for a very long time."

"I'll buy you gold and diamonds, sweetheart," he said.

"I don't need gold and diamonds," she said in a soft voice.

"What do you need?" he whispered.

The longing in her slanted eyes filled him with a desperate yearning and hope. She dropped her gaze. He knew not to push her.

He reached out a hand and tucked a stray curl behind her ear. "Your hair looks incredible swept up like that." He smiled. "But I still prefer it loose."

She returned his smile. "And after all the money I spent on this hairdo."

Mary Beth took a deep breath when the limo pulled up to the massive Tudor-style mansion. Once owned by one of Delaware's richest families, the house was now used for charity events, weddings, and dances. Her graduation formal had been held here. She pressed her hand to her stomach to stop its quivering. *I can do this. I can do this.*

The driver opened the limo door to help her out of the luxurious vehicle. Part of her wanted to step back inside the warm cocoon of the car, where she and Tom could stay locked away from the prying eyes of the world.

"Ready?" Tom held his arm out.

"Sure," she said, forcing a smile and slipping her arm through his.

When they reached the wide marble stairs guarded by stone lions, she hesitated. Apprehension balled in her chest. The last time she'd walked up these stairs she'd been a starry-eyed innocent. She'd felt like Cinderella then, the poor girl dressed in pretty finery with Prince Charming by her side. Midnight had ended the fantasy. Would the same happen tonight?

Tom put his hand over hers where it rested in the crook of his arm. "Relax, Cat Eyes. I can feel your tension. You're with me. I'll take care of you."

She chewed her lip. Would he take care of her, or would he desert her for his own kind, like so long ago?

"I'm okay, Tom," she said, forcing a smile. "The place hasn't changed. I always thought it looked like a fairy castle with all the tiny white lights in the windows and trees."

His hand tightened over hers. "Mary Beth, I didn't realize . . . I hadn't thought."

She shrugged. "That was in another life. It means nothing now."

"Doesn't it?" He narrowed his eyes. His blue gaze probed hers.

She glanced quickly away. "Let's go in," she said.

Once inside the antique-filled foyer, an attendant took her wrap and showed them to a small receiving line where richly dressed men and women waited to greet their hosts. Feeling more like Cinderella by the minute, Mary Beth widened her eyes at their surroundings, even more lavish than she'd remembered.

Stairs of white marble shot with gold led down to the elaborate ballroom. Gilt carvings decorated the soft ivory walls. Gold velvet curtains swathed the floor-to-ceiling windows.

Couples of all ages danced to a rock song played by the orchestra at the far end of the long room. The exquisite clothing of the elegant guests, the décor, and the tuxedoed wait-staff reeked of money. Lots of money.

She felt Tom looking at her and gave him a smile. He took her hand in his. She squared her shoulders. Because of him she belonged here. He made her feel special wherever they went. He'd grown from a spoiled boy to a man with no social pretense. Pride and love for him swirled in a heady mix in her heart.

Tom introduced her to their hosts. The couple, international jet-setters, owned half the state and an island in the Bahamas. The husband greeted them warmly, but the wife's knowing gaze scrutinized Mary Beth from her upswept hair to her stiletto sandals. Mary Beth could almost hear the *ka-ching* of the cash register in the woman's head as she assessed her net worth.

After several uncomfortable minutes of small talk, Tom led her down the wide stairs to the ballroom. The band had just started a romantic slow tune.

"Dance with me," he said.

She settled into his arms, losing herself in the security of his masculine strength.

"Don't let Roxanne get to you," he said, nodding toward their hostess. "She's like that with everyone. She married into money and she likes to flaunt it."

Mary Beth glanced up at him with a wry smile. "I think she figured out exactly how much is in my bank account. And it didn't meet her approval."

He laughed and pulled her closer. "Sweetheart, you're richer in more ways than she'll ever be."

With his words warming her, she leaned her head against his broad chest, breathing in his unique scent of citrus and musk that she knew so well. For a few seconds she allowed herself the fantasy that the formal hadn't ended in disaster, that she'd spent the last twelve years loving Tom, having his children. . . . She pressed her eyes shut. Her life had taken a different turn and she was stronger for it. Just as her love for Tom was stronger and deeper now.

"You always feel so good," he said, brushing his lips on her temple. "I like your new perfume."

She smiled and snuggled into the warmth of his arms, glad that he liked the scent that she'd picked out just for him.

A familiar, brittle laugh cut into her pleasure. Chills raced up her spine. She lifted her head and glanced to the side. Taylor Bennett, elegant in navy velvet, glided by in the arms of a heavyset, balding man. The familiar cleft in the man's chin stirred up an uneasy feeling in Mary Beth, like a bad dream that she couldn't quite recall.

Taylor narrowed her ice blue eyes at Mary Beth as they passed. The man looked over at her, then bent his head to whisper in the blond's ear. They stared at Mary Beth and laughed before moving away.

The arrogance of Taylor and her partner, the meanness that hardened their eyes provoked memories that made sweat form on Mary Beth's palms.

Faces from the past swam in her mind. Four years of taunts, ridicule, and cruel jokes rushed at her, drowning her in a sea of insecurities and pain.

Stop it, she told herself. She had determined to put aside the old fears and uncertainties. For Tom's sake. For her own sake. She had every reason to hold her head up high. She'd come a long way. And she had done it on her own.

The music ended and she and Tom drew apart. He reached out a hand to brush a strand of hair off her face. "Why so quiet?" he said. "I hope you're having a good time." The concern on his handsome face made warmth spiral through her.

"I always have a good time when I'm with you," she said, surprised at the easy truth that slipped from her lips.

He took her hand in his. "Do you mean that, Mary Beth? Sometimes I wonder."

"Wonder what?"

"If you really want to be with me." His deep blue eyes searched hers.

"Tom, if you only knew." She wanted to bite the words back. If he started asking questions she might be tempted to tell him how much she loved him. And if he rejected her, or worse, took pity on her, what would she do?

He took her chin in his hand. "Tell me what I should know. What's in that beautiful head of yours?"

"Food," she said, forcing a lightness she didn't feel. "Have a drink." She grabbed two crystal goblets filled with water from a passing waiter and handed one to him.

He arched an eyebrow and tapped his glass to hers. "To the truth. You can't run from me forever, Cat Eyes."

"I don't know what you mean," she said, locking her gaze with his.

"You're a terrible liar," he said, laughing. "Come on. Let's find the food. We'll talk later."

In the forty-five minutes it took for them to reach the buffet tables, Mary Beth felt truly famished. Half the guests must have stopped Tom as they made their way out of the ballroom. Most were business associates. Some were former classmates who pretended not to recognize her until Tom introduced them. All made no attempt to hide their curiosity as they openly studied her.

She'd certainly picked the right venue to make their affair public, she thought, as anxiety tightened her stomach. But Tom's attentiveness toward her in front of his friends and acquaintances dissolved some of her fears.

"At last," she said when they reached the huge dining room, where massive white-clothed tables were heaped with enough food to feed a small nation.

She grabbed Tom's hand and squeezed it. "We spent months coordinating this dinner and cooking a good deal of it. We hired chefs from the best restaurants in three states. What if no one likes the food?"

"Look around you," Tom said. "There are more people here than on the dance floor. And the music's great."

She glanced around the room. Long lines of chattering, laughing guests queued up at tables where chefs carved slabs of tender beef, turkey, and ham. She and Gail had seen to it that only the best cuts were used. White-gloved servers stood ready to dish out a cornucopia of fresh vegetables, flown in from all over the world.

A centerpiece of King Neptune reigned over seafood of every kind, from succulent shrimp to fat lobster tails.

"I don't know where to begin," she said, looking up at Tom. "Maybe I should go into the kitchen first and see how Gail is doing."

"Oh, no you don't," he said, cupping her elbow and propelling her toward the seafood. "She's got enough under-chefs and servers to stock a palace. I'm sure she's fine. You're staying with me. Besides, if I let you out of my sight, some other guy will try to claim you."

She stumbled to a stop. "What?"

He traced his finger over her lips. "You're easily the most beautiful woman here. I've seen the way men look at you."

Heat spread from her neck to her face. "You're imagining that."

"You don't get it, do you?" he said, shaking his head. "That's part of your appeal. You don't see yourself as others see you and you don't like being the center of attention. You sure intimidated me in school."

"Now you're joking," she said, laughing.

He studied her with a serious gaze. "I'm not, but I'll tell you all about that some other time. If we don't get in line now there won't be any lobster left."

After filling their plates with a variety of seafood, they wandered into an enclosed sunroom where small wrought iron tables had been set up.

Old classmates and prominent city residents, some of them her clients, were seated at surrounding tables, but no one approached them. Mary Beth felt their stares, but she ignored them. She focused all her attention on the man who had brought her, the man who treated her with a subtle reverence, as if he were proud to be with her.

Maybe Tom cared for her after all. Fear, like a silent intruder, crept in. All her life, whenever she'd felt happy, something bad happened. She didn't dare dream.

"You're quiet again," he said.

"I'm just enjoying this wonderful food. I hear the caterers are the best in the city."

He smiled. "And beautiful. Especially the redhead. She means a lot to me."

"She does?" Mary Beth almost choked on the Clams Casino she was eating. She washed the food down with lemon water.

"When did they start letting the kitchen help eat with the guests?" Taylor's arrogant voice made Mary Beth stiffen. She swung around. Taylor pushed a chair away from the table next to them. The sound of wrought iron scraping flagstone pierced the air. The blond and her date settled at the table.

"Taylor, I thought you had more class than that," Tom said in a tight voice. "Apologize to Mary Beth."

"Calm down, Sackett," Taylor's escort said. His mocking laugh made chills skitter along Mary Beth's spine.

She stared at the paunchy, pale-faced man. He leered at her. Recognition hit her like a painful bout of food poisoning.

McKee Wright. Crueler than all the others in the school. When they were sophomores she'd reported him for bullying a younger student. He'd never forgiven her. He'd tried to kiss her once the following year. She'd kicked him in the groin. After that his vindictiveness knew no bounds.

He'd gained a lot of weight and lost the thick curly hair that had been his pride. But his eyes were the same—hard and mean.

Tom put his hand over Mary Beth's. She smiled at him, acknowledging his support. Her gratitude for his defense was ready to burst from her heart.

"Wright, stay out of this," Tom said. A muscle clenched in his jaw. "Taylor owes Mary Beth an apology."

The other man snickered. "Still walking on the wild side, Sackett? Can't say I blame you. The little cook is a tasty tidbit. Her kiss packs a real wallop, as I recall."

Tom jumped up, knocking over their table. The porcelain dishes flew off to shatter on the stone floor.

All conversation and movement ceased. The stares of the others in the room pierced Mary Beth like daggers.

Tom grabbed McKee's collar and jerked him out of his chair. He raised his fist, aiming at the other man's face.

"No, Tom. Don't." Mary Beth pulled at Tom's arm, stopping him.

Still holding onto McKee, Tom turned his gaze to Mary Beth. His labored breathing and the anger that burned in his eyes made her flinch.

"He's not worth it, Tom." She looked at the other man. His skin had turned gray and his eyes bulged from the choke hold Tom had on his shirt.

"You're pathetic, McKee," Mary Beth said. She swung her gaze to Taylor, standing behind her. "You're both pathetic." The blond's heavily made-up eyes widened in shock.

Mary Beth released Tom's arm, and with a final look of disgust at Taylor and McKee, she marched from the room.

"Now it's my turn," she heard Tom say. "You sicken. . . ."

Slowing her step, Mary Beth smiled. Despite the fact that she'd probably lost some potential wealthy clients, she felt as if a hand had reached down from heaven and plucked the weight of years off her shoulders.

She was truly free of the past. She knew that Taylor, McKee, and the rest of their crowd were petty-minded jerks, but she actually felt sorry for them now. Tom had never been as mean, except for that one time, but he'd grown and changed. And she loved him for it.

She wound her way through the noisy crowd as tears of relief and worry filled her eyes. Why hadn't Tom followed her? For his sake, she hoped he wasn't fighting with McKee.

The band started a loud disco tune. She winced at the high pitch of the music. Like Cinderella, she wanted to run from the ball, but she wouldn't leave without Tom. Not after he'd come to her defense. So different from the last time. She'd collect her wrap and find the limo driver and wait for him in the car.

"Mary Beth," Tom yelled.

Her heart soared at the sound of his voice. She pivoted to face him. He walked quickly toward her, his face grim. He had loosened his tie and a wayward curl fell over his forehead. She wanted to throw herself in his arms and tell him how much she loved him, but she'd caused enough of a scene already tonight.

The crowd, suddenly quiet, parted for him. Even the couples on the dance floor slowed to watch them. Mary Beth's face burned and she looked straight ahead, not daring to look around.

"Thank God I found you." Tom gripped her shoulders. "I was afraid you'd gone, but I had to tell those two exactly what I thought of them." He smiled. "That felt good."

She couldn't stop her own grin. "Let's get out of here."

"Not until we talk."

"Not here," she said, sliding her gaze to some of the guests who were openly staring at them. Her face grew hotter.

"Come on," he said. He led her out of the ballroom and through the entry hall. Small groups of people milled around the large foyer.

When he headed toward the carpeted stairs that led to the upper floors, she pulled back. "I just want to go home," she said.

He shook his head. "Later." He took her hand and gently pulled her up the stairs.

"Where are we going?" she asked.

"Someplace where we can be alone. I know this house. Don't worry. No one will bother us." He turned and grinned at her. "I think after my little display on the patio, no one would dare mess with me right now."

She laughed despite her jittery stomach.

When they reached the second floor, he ushered her through ornately carved double doors into a cavernous room filled with heavy leather furniture and empty bookshelves.

"The library," he said. "They sold the books a long time ago."

"Tom, I don't. . . ."

"Sit down," he said, gesturing toward a burgundy sofa.

"I don't feel like sitting," she said.

He let out an exasperated sigh. "Sit." He pushed her gently onto the couch.

He stood over her, his blue eyes blazing. "We are going to have that talk we should have had a long time ago."

"But. . . ."

He held his hand up. "Just be quiet, Cat Eyes. I have something that I've waited years to say and I want to get it out before I lose my nerve."

She sat on the edge of the cushion, her hands clasped tightly on her lap. Her gaze took in the lines of fatigue and stress around his mouth. He'd laid his reputation as a community and business leader on the line for her tonight. What happened all those years ago no longer mattered. She wanted to hold him, smooth away the worry from his face. Tell him how much he meant to her.

He ran his hand over his eyes. When he looked at her again, regret filled his features. "We need to talk about that night twelve years ago," he said.

"It's okay, Tom," she said.

He shook his head. "No, it's not. Let me finish."

He was right. They had to talk.

His gaze locked with hers. "I was so angry with you for running away from me at the graduation formal, Mary Beth."

She sucked in her breath. "Angry at me? I'm the one who was humiliated. By you. By your friends."

He raked his fingers through his hair. "I was angry because I knew you felt insecure about dating me. I thought I had finally earned your trust. You proved me wrong. You were so ready to believe the worst of me that you ran off without giving me a chance."

Indignation stiffened her. She glared at him. "You're blaming me?"

The tendons along his neck were taut. "No, I'm bungling this whole deposition. This is tough." He began pacing the worn Oriental carpet.

He faced her from across the room. "I was angry at first. Later I realized that my own cowardice kept me from chasing after you. I was such a jerk."

"I–I loved you so much," she said. "Why did you set me up?"

His face paled. "Set you up? Is that what you believed all these years, that I had something to do with what happened?"

She widened her eyes and nodded. A lump formed in her throat. She couldn't speak, couldn't breathe. She fingered the silver bracelet she wore, the one she'd thrown in her jewel box that night. All this time she'd been so sure. . . .

He crossed the room in quick strides to sit beside her. He grabbed her shoulders, forcing her to look at him.

"Sweetheart, I may have been a wretched coward, but I had no part in what they did."

She blinked as his words penetrated her brain. "You–you didn't?" Relief brought tears to her eyes.

He wiped a tear off her cheek with his thumb. "I'm just as guilty for standing by while they hurt you. Yes, I was upset that you had so little faith in me, but I knew if I defended you they'd laugh at me too. And I thought I needed them."

His features softened and he skimmed his finger over her lips. "I needed you, but I was too self-involved to see that. Can you ever forgive me?"

She drew a deep breath. "I forgave you a long time ago, but I didn't realize it till tonight."

"Cat Eyes," he whispered. He brushed his lips over hers in a whisper of a kiss.

She wanted to hug him to her, to declare her love,

but unanswered questions hovered in the air between them. They needed to start their future with a clean plate.

"Tom," she said, drawing away. "Why didn't you call me later and explain? You hurt me so much that night."

"I'm so sorry, sweetheart," he said, stroking her cheek. "I called after I got back from Boston but your line was disconnected. I telephoned your friends, Maria and Liz, but they hung up on me."

"They never told me," she said. "Mom and I were at the beach with my aunt for the summer." She frowned. "What do you mean after you got back from Boston?"

"You know. My dad. The accident."

She shook her head. "What accident?"

A bitter laugh escaped him. "I can't believe this." He leveled his gaze at her. "Mary Beth, my dad was in a bad car accident in Boston. The night of the dance. I got the message soon after you ran out. My family and I left for Boston right away."

"I never knew," she said, chewing her lip.

He cupped her face. "That night changed me. I almost lost my dad. I'd lost you. I was such a spoiled, selfish kid. And I hurt the ones who cared for me the most. I decided to turn my life around, to make amends to all the people I'd disappointed. The storefront law practice was one of the things I did to ease my conscience."

He took her hands in his. "I never really forgot you

and I never stopped regretting that I let you down. The more time that went by, the harder it became to find you and ask your forgiveness."

He released her hands to comb his fingers through his hair. "I eased my guilt by telling myself you'd forgotten me and what I did and were probably happily married with a couple of kids. That last thought bothered me most of all."

"It did?" She pressed a trembling hand against her stomach. "I'm having a hard time digesting all of this." She took a calming breath. "There's something else I have to know."

"Anything," he said, leaning back. "No more secrets between us. Ever."

She clasped her hands together. "Did you buy my business to atone for the past? Was it charity after all?" She chewed her lip, afraid of the answer. But she needed the truth.

"No, Cat Eyes," he said, straightening. "It wasn't charity. I would have found another way to make things up to you. Sure, I saw your problem as an opportunity to earn your forgiveness, but investing in your company was a solid financial decision. I wouldn't have done it otherwise."

She gave him a shaky smile. "You saved Kendrick and Company. I'll always be grateful."

He took her hands and kissed each palm. "I want a lot more than gratitude from you, Mary Beth."

Her heart beat like a wild bird trapped in a cage. "What do you want, Tom?"

"You," he said.

Tears stung her eyes and hope rose up in her chest. She stared into the blue depths of his eyes, unable to look away.

Still holding her hands, his gaze searched hers. "I have something more to say. It's not easy for me. Hear me out. Okay?"

She nodded.

"I thought I loved Clarice," he said, his voice low and serious. "Her and Jack's betrayal stung badly, but on another level, I felt relieved. I had begun to realize that something was missing from my life. Something important.

"This feeling of unfinished business nagged at me. My family wanted me home. Clarice and Jack sure didn't need me. And running into Max Cummings in Manhattan clinched it."

"Max Cummings?" she said, blinking as if cold water had been sprinkled on her face. "I catered his son's christening. What does he have to do with anything?"

"He told me you were a caterer," Tom said. "But more importantly, he mentioned you were single. That's when I knew I had to come home."

"Because I wasn't married?" she said, barely able to believe her ears.

He caressed her with his gaze. "If you weren't married, it meant I still had a chance." His mouth spread into a slow grin that made her breath catch in her throat. "But that wasn't the reason I gave myself for coming home."

"It wasn't?" she whispered.

He shook his head. "I've been in denial for years. The truth has been jumping up and down in front of me like a nervous litigator, but I ignored it. I told myself I wanted your forgiveness, then your friendship. Maybe I was afraid of being hurt again. Or maybe I figured you'd never care for me after what I did."

"Care for you?" Now her heart had stopped for sure.

"When I looked at you tonight, I knew," he said, holding her hands tightly. "You are so beautiful, so radiant, and I need you in my life. I love you, Mary Beth. I've always loved you."

"Oh, God, Tom." Tears streamed down her face.

He stroked her cheeks, wiping her tears away. "You said something a while ago about loving me before. Is there a chance that you can learn to love me again?" His eyes, filled with pain and uncertainty, searched hers.

She threw her arms around him and buried her face in his neck.

"I love you so much," she said, sobbing. "I thought you couldn't possibly love me."

He pulled away and cupped her face in his hands. Joy had replaced the pain in his eyes. "You love me?"

"Yes, yes, a thousand times yes." She laughed.

He kissed her then, a kiss filled with desire and promise. She wrapped her arms around his neck and kissed him with all the fervor and love that she'd held inside for so many years.

She knew that no matter what happened in their life together, they'd always have the passion, and the love, to see them through.

He pulled away to stare into her eyes. "Marry me, Mary Beth. As soon as possible."

She nodded. "I'd marry you tonight if I could."

He laughed and grazed her lips with his finger. "I'm going to spend the rest of my life loving you, Cat Eyes."

She took his hand and kissed his palm. "We'll spend the rest of our lives loving each other. Let's go home, Tom."

"Not yet," he said, standing. He grabbed her hand and pulled her gently up. "First, we're going back to that ball and I'm announcing to everyone that the beautiful, intelligent Mary Beth Kendrick has made me the happiest man in the world."